BRODY

Susan Fisher-Davis

Men of Clifton, Montana
Book 3

Brody
2

Erotic Romance
Brody
Copyright © 2015 Susan Fisher-Davis
First Print book Publication: March 2015
Cover design by Amy Valentini
Edited by Susan Toth
Proofread by Renee Waring
ISBN: 9798706168131
All cover art copyright © 2015 by Susan Davis

ALL RIGHTS RESERVED: This literary work may not be reproduced or transmitted in any form or by any means, including electronic or photographic reproduction, in whole or in part, without express written permission.

All characters and events in this book are fictitious. Any resemblance to actual persons living or dead is strictly coincidental.

Blue Whiskey Publishing
Susan Davis
www.susanfisherdavisauthor.weebly.com

Dedication

A big thank you to my readers. It's because of you that I do this.
My husband, Rob for staying away when I'm in my cave. I love you.
Thank you, Toby S., for being a wonderful friend, confidant, and listener.

Brody
4

Chapter One

Brody Morgan rode his Harley down Main Street and ignored the stares. Five years ago, he'd left Clifton, Montana, vowing never to return. They couldn't know it was him behind the smoked visor but the glares made him think differently. He mentally shook his head. The people of Clifton would have a field day once they found out he was back and going to be working for the Sheriff's department.

Brody grunted. Him as a deputy? They'd laugh their heads off. But, he needed a job and the sheriff, Sam Garrett, needed a deputy. Sam was a good friend. They'd worked together at the US Marshal's office in Butte but had been friends growing up in Clifton. They talked regularly and when Brody told Sam he'd left the Marshals, Sam offered him a job. Brody hated the idea of returning to Clifton, but he didn't have much of a choice. He was going to clean up his parents' home and live there until he decided what he wanted to do with the rest of his life. He was thirty-two and should have kids by now. A beautiful redhead clouded his vision. Brody shook his head to clear it. She was the reason he never wanted to come back and he wasn't looking forward to seeing her again. He'd broken her heart when he left and she'd never forgive him. She'd shouted it at him when he rode away on his bike. The June sun beat down on him as he rode down Main Street. His eyes scanned the sidewalks crowded with people. *What the hell was going on?* He remembered the sidewalks as being empty even during the Christmas season but now, people moved along them, going in and out of the shops. Brody came to a stop at the intersection and stared at the people crossing the street in front of him. There was only one main street through Clifton with one stop light. Tall brick buildings stood on each side. His head moved to the other side and there were just as many people over there too. Was there something going on he didn't know about? Sam hadn't mentioned anything when they spoke last week. Mentally shaking his head, he moved the bike forward when the light changed to green. He could feel the sweat trickling between his shoulder blades and down his spine. The leather he wore had him sweating in the summer but it was necessary to a biker, no matter how hot the weather. It was a safety issue, not a fashion statement.

He pulled into the Sheriff's Department parking lot and shut off the bike. Straddling it, he removed his helmet and glanced around. No one paid him any mind. Sighing, he swung his leg over the bike, strode to the doors, and walked inside. It was much cooler inside than the heat outside. Brody glanced to his right and saw an older woman staring at him. She slowly stood.

"Brody Morgan as I live and breathe," she huffed.

Brody frowned at her and then recognition dawned. "Betty Lou Harper?"

Betty Lou cackled. "It is." She came around

the counter faster than a woman her size should be able. She grabbed him and hugged him. "You look so good, honey. It's good to have you home again."

Brody leaned down to hug her. She barely reached his shoulder. "It's good to see you too."

"What are you doing here?"

"I'm here to see Sam. Is he in?"

Betty Lou shook her head. "He ran down to the diner to pick up lunch. He'll be back in a few minutes. Have a seat in the waiting room. It's much cooler in here."

Brody nodded and took a seat in the room across the hall. The old black and white tiles on the floor showed scuffmarks from years of wear. The red plastic chairs sat along a wall. He set his helmet on the chair beside him and ran his fingers through his black hair. Stretching his long legs out in front of him, he clasped his hands together over his flat stomach and leaned his head back against the wall while he waited for Sam.

A few minutes later, Brody jerked when someone kicked his foot. He jumped up from the chair, ready for a fight. Sam Garrett stood in front of him glaring.

"I see you're as ugly as ever, Garrett," Brody growled.

"Same to you, Morgan."

The two men stared at each other, then laughed and hugged. "Damn, it's good to see you Brody. Come on back to my office." Sam led the way.

Brody watched as Sam took his Stetson off

and hung it up before moving behind the old wooden desk and sitting down. He nodded for Brody to take a seat. Sam leaned back in his chair, folded his arms across his broad chest, and stared at Brody.

Brody shifted in the chair. "Christ, Sam. You're making me feel like I'm in the fucking principal's office."

"Good. Because in a way you are. I'm your boss. You won't get to slide by. I'll ride your ass just as I do the other two deputies I have. Are we clear on that?"

"Crystal," Brody growled out the word.

"Good. I'll get the paperwork." Sam stood. "Betty Lou, I need…"

"I already have it, Sam." Betty Lou stood in the doorway with the paperwork.

Sam muttered under his breath making Brody chuckle, but he straightened in the chair when Sam glared at him.

"Here, fill this out. I'll need you on night shift. Is that a problem?"

"Would it matter, Sam? I'm fine with it." Brody reached into his shirt pocket, pulled out a pair of glasses, and put them on.

"You still wear glasses? No contacts?" Sam asked.

"I can't stick those damn things in my eyes. Never could," Brody mumbled.

Sam laughed. "I understand. I hate putting drops in."

Brody ran his hand over his mouth. "Me, too. I've always been like that. Too late to change now."

Brody

Sam nodded. "Once you're finished, just give the paperwork to Betty Lou. You can start tomorrow night. I'll get you a few shirts. I'll have to order more. Just wear jeans. You have your own weapon, right?" At Brody's nod, Sam continued. "Not much goes on in this town but be careful when you check out Dewey's bar. It can get rowdy and with all the tourists in town, it could be worse."

"Tourists? What are they here to see?" Brody frowned.

"There's a bed and breakfast just outside of town now. Hattie Daniels' place."

"Hattie turned her ranch into a bed and breakfast?" Brody couldn't fathom it.

Sam puckered his brow. "Hattie passed away over a year ago. Her granddaughter Becca inherited it and turned it into the Clifton B and B. Becca also married Jake Stone."

"Wait. What? Are you serious? Jake got married?" Brody was stunned.

Sam grinned. "Not only Jake, but Gabe's married too."

"Gabe Stone is married?" Brody shook his head.

"He married Emma Conner. They have a gorgeous little girl. Sophie."

"I think I made a mistake coming back here. There must be something in the water."

Sam shook his head. "It's love. Plain and simple."

"What about Riley? Have you heard from him?"

"Not for about a year. The last I heard he was

retiring. Thirty-two and retiring. He made a killing in real estate and he also owns a huge beef ranch in Texas."

"I haven't talked to him either. He won't come back here, that's for sure. Not as long as his dad is alive." Brody sighed. "He hates the bastard and who can blame him?"

Sam shook his head. "I'd love to see him though. It's been too long."

"You married, Sam?"

"Oh, hell no." Sam shook his head. "Not gonna happen."

Brody laughed and filled out the paperwork and rose from the chair. He stuck his hand out. "Thanks Sam. I appreciate this."

"No problem. I needed another man. You came along at the right time." Sam tilted his head. "Are you going to see Madilyn?"

"No way in hell. She'd slit my throat." Brody shuddered.

"You'd deserve it," Sam muttered.

"Jesus, I know Sam. What I did to her was wrong but it was a long time ago."

Sam snorted. "Not so long ago she's forgotten." He sighed. "I have to get back to work. I'll see you here tomorrow night. I'm here seven to seven. Come in at six thirty. I'll introduce you to Rick and Mark then. Once you get into a rhythm, I'll straighten out the shifts so we all won't work such long hours."

Brody gave him a terse nod. "I'm going to head to the ranch."

"Are you staying there?"

"Yes. Mom and dad haven't been there in two

years. I know it's going to need some cleaning but I'll take care of it. A thousand acres allows for some great privacy. I might even get a few Angus again."

"It's certainly prime enough for them." Sam strolled toward the door. "Any questions, call me." He handed Brody a card and left.

Brody sighed and left the office. He stopped at Betty Lou's desk. "How long have you been working here, Betty Lou?"

"Since Sam became Sheriff last November. He beat Walt Jefferson by a landslide." She sniffed. "His mama asked him to hire me. That's why I'm here."

Brody chuckled. "Trust me, Betty Lou, if Sam didn't want you here, you wouldn't be here." He shrugged. "I've known him a long time. He's a straight shooter. I've never known him to lie to make someone feel better. He tells it like it is." Brody leaned over the counter. "You should know that." After giving her a smile, he strolled outside, hopped on his motorcycle, and headed for the ranch.

* * * *

Madilyn Young stared at the motorcycle as it passed the shop where she worked. A shiver ran down her spine. Dear God, please no. Don't let it be him.

"Madilyn? Are you all right?"

"I...yes, Katie. I'm fine." *Liar!* Madilyn turned to face her boss and friend, Kaitlyn Parker. "I just thought I saw someone I used to know."

"I've never understood that, 'someone I used to know'. You still know them." Kaitlyn frowned.

Madilyn laughed. "That's true. I don't think it was him, though."

"Did you think it was Brody?" Kaitlyn smiled at her.

"I'm sure it wasn't him." Madilyn hoped it wasn't anyway. She wasn't ready for him to come back yet. Who was she kidding? She'd never be ready.

Kaitlyn snorted. "Sam hasn't said anything lately about him coming back."

Madilyn smiled sadly. "I know but I'm hoping he doesn't come back. Ever."

Kaitlyn nodded. "You never know. I'm going to head home since we close in fifteen minutes. You can lock up." She gave a little wave. "I'll see you tomorrow."

Madilyn nodded and took a seat at the counter. She loved working at Clifton's Florist and Greenhouse. Katie was a great florist and Madilyn had a green thumb when it came to tropical plants. When the shop opened five years ago, Madilyn was at the door asking for a job. Katie was the manager and with Brody gone from her life, Madilyn needed to do something to keep her occupied. It hadn't helped for the longest time, then the years fell away and Madilyn was finally able to put him to the back of her mind, but he would forever be in her heart. *Damn you, Brody Morgan!* Madilyn blinked back tears. Five years later and he could still make her cry. When the bell above the door rang, she glanced over to see Sam Garrett, Katie's brother and the local Sheriff, walk in. Her heart gave a little skip. Sam was one sexy man. He stood six foot five with a hard body. Dark brown, almost black, hair, and he had the most amazing blue eyes. They were beautiful. She inwardly sighed. No matter how gorgeous Sam was, Madilyn had never been interested in him. Brody Morgan owned her heart.

"Hi, Madilyn. Is Katie around?"

"She left a few minutes ago," Madilyn told him.

Sam nodded. "All right. I'll talk with her later." He smiled. "How are you?"

Madilyn smiled at him. She liked Sam. His smile was beautiful. *Jesus, Madilyn! Why can't you go for Sam?* "I'm good, Sam. What about you?"

"I'm good." He glanced around. "Well, I better get going. Take care, Madilyn." He headed for the door.

"Sam…"

He turned to face her and raised an eyebrow when she didn't say anything. Madilyn cleared her throat. "Is…is he back?" she whispered and watched as Sam swore softly. She had her answer.

"Yes. He'll be on nightshift." Sam sighed. "I told you there was a chance he would come back."

Madilyn nodded. "I don't want to see him, Sam." Her voice sounded like rust.

"I understand. You probably won't since he's on nights. During the day, he'll be sleeping and when he's off, he'll be at the ranch, cleaning it up."

"He's staying out there? He always said he hated it."

Brody

14

"He hated it because he felt he was stuck there for years before he joined the Marshals." Sam shrugged. "He was young and wanted out. We all did."

"I know." Madilyn was trying her best not break down. How could she face him again? Clifton was a small town and everyone knew everyone else's business. She was sure they all remembered the night Brody Morgan left her.

Sam hugged her. "It'll be all right. It was a long time ago, Madilyn."

She nodded and watched Sam stroll away. He didn't understand. No one did. Madilyn Young would forever love Brody Morgan. He'd taken her virginity and her heart. Madilyn thought back to the night he told her he was joining the U S Marshals.

"No. Brody, please. You can't," Madilyn pleaded.

"It's what I want to do. After listening to Sam talk about it, it's what I want to do," Brody repeated emphatically.

"You know how I feel about law enforcement. I'm scared to death you'll be killed like my dad was."

"I'm already in law enforcement. Your dad let down his guard and you know it. I won't do that." Brody tried to take her hand, she jerked back from him.

"It doesn't matter if he let his guard down or not. He died in the line of duty and you could too. You know I hate that you still work for the Police department. Brody, please. Don't do this to me. You said you loved me." Madilyn's tears rolled

Brody

down her face.

"Baby, please don't cry. I do love you. Come with me, Maddie."

"No! I will not go with you and watch you die. Being in the Marshals is too dangerous," she shouted.

Brody stared at her. "You're going to throw away what we have?"

"No. You are." Madilyn moved away from him. "If you leave I will never forgive you. Do you hear me, Brody Morgan? I will *never* forgive you," she yelled.

"I won't be back, Madilyn. Once I leave, it's over for us unless you come with me."

Madilyn shook her head. "I won't go with you." She wiped tears away. "I will never forgive you. You know how I feel about it."

Brody strode to his bike. "I guess you'll never forgive me then." He put his helmet on, started his bike, and roared off into the night.

Now he was back. She would never get the image of him riding away out of her mind. She'd been twenty-two and he'd been twenty-seven. Brody went to college and obtained a Bachelor's Degree, then worked for four years in the local Police Department with Madilyn's father. Arthur Young pulled a speeder over from out of state and the man shot Arthur for no reason other than being angry about it. It had torn Madilyn apart. Her mother had died when she was five years old. Her father was all she had until Brody came into her life. She pleaded with Brody to leave the department but she never dreamed he'd accept a position with the Marshals. Sam had joined the Marshals right after college, and once Brody talked with him, he'd made the decision to join them too.

Madilyn put her hands over her face. How could she face him? The time would come when she'd see him. There was no doubt in her mind about it. They would run into each other. Maybe in the five years he'd been gone, he'd gotten ugly and fat. She grunted. Brody had always taken care of his body. She groaned. *God!* What a body he'd had. Solid pecs, hard biceps, and a six-pack stomach. Madilyn had loved his thick black hair and brown eyes. She even loved seeing him wear his glasses. He didn't wear them often but when he did, he looked so sexy, and she wasn't the only woman to think that way. The women in town thought it looked sexy too. But he'd loved Madilyn and told her he wanted to marry her. Until the night he informed her he was joining the Marshals in Butte.

Madilyn moved to the door and locked it. She then counted the money and took care of the credit card receipts. When she was done, she locked up and walked home. Her apartment sat in the new complex two blocks from the shop. Her heart stopped when she heard the roar of a motorcycle coming toward her and she sighed with relief when it rode on past her. Her relief was short-lived, however, when she heard it coming back up behind her. Madilyn refused to glance back. The bike roared by her, turned around in the middle of the street, and came back toward her. It pulled in front of her on the sidewalk. She stopped and held her breath as the

Brody

17

rider removed his helmet. Madilyn bit her lip to hold back a groan when she saw his gorgeous face. Brody Morgan hadn't gotten worse with age. He'd gotten better. The maturity in his face made him sexier. The crow's feet at the corners of his eyes were even sexy. Those brown eyes stared at her from behind his glasses.

"Hello Madilyn," he said softly.

A shiver shot through her. His voice seemed deeper. Taking a deep breath, she stared at him.

"Hello Brody." Then she strolled around his bike and continued down the sidewalk.

* * * *

Brody watched her walk away from him. Damn, she looked good. She was even more beautiful than before. Madilyn was a tall, gorgeous redhead with porcelain skin. Thick, lush eyelashes surrounding light green luminous eyes. He'd always loved those eyes and her light red hair. She had the temper to go with it. Brody watched her disappear into the apartment complex. Firing up the bike, he headed home. Why he turned around and rode back to her was anyone's guess. He'd thought he was seeing things when he rode down the street and spotted her. Brody should have just kept going. All seeing her again did was make him realize how much he still loved her. The time would come when they'd have to talk and he wasn't looking forward to it.

When Brody pulled up to the house, he stayed seated on the bike and glanced around, taking it all in. The two red barns were still in good condition but the small hay barn looked as if a gust of wind would topple it. The grass in the front yard of the house was tall and the rose bushes his mother had meticulously cared for were growing out of control. There were so many memories rushing back to him. Horses used to fill the now empty corrals and the thousand acres of pasture had been filled with the best Angus beef money could buy. His gaze swept to the hayloft where he and Madilyn would sneak to make love. How many times had they made love there?

Brody's parents loved her as if she was their own and she'd loved them in return. Swinging his leg over the bike, he strode to the back door and unlocked it with the key his mother had sent him. The musty smell made him wrinkle his nose as he entered the kitchen. His parents really should have hired someone to take care of the place since they refused to sell it. Brody went to the window above the sink and opened it. A light breeze moved the sheer curtains. His gaze ran the room. A sheet covered the center island. The copper pots and pans above it hung covered with dust. Dust coated the red countertops and the white cupboards looked dull. The white appliances also lacked luster. Cherry hardwood floors no longer gleamed. Brody's mother had kept them glowing. It would shock her to see them now. Taking a deep breath, he headed down the hallway to the living room. All of the furniture had sheets over it. He walked toward the fireplace, squatted down, looked up the flue, and sighed. Thank God, the damper remained closed. That's all he would need is bats coming

Brody

in. Striding to the windows, he drew the drapes open to let the sunlight pour in. Dust motes danced in the beams. He pulled the sheets down from the two windows on each side of the fireplace and started to cough when the dust floated down to him. Pulling the sheet off the couch, he took a seat. It was going to take a while to get it cleaned up and he would need to build a new hay barn if he was serious about getting beef again. He had the money to do it and his parents were all for it. He remembered the conversation with them two weeks ago.

"Will you eventually tell us what happened?" his mother asked.

"One day, mom. Not just yet."

"Does Sam know?" His dad wanted to know.

Brody sighed. "No, dad. Not yet."

"You'll stay at the ranch." It wasn't a question from his mother but more of a demand.

Brody chuckled. "Yes. I wouldn't mind getting it up and running again."

His dad laughed. "Well, if you do, we'd be more than happy to let you."

"We'll give you the ranch, Brody," his mother said softly.

"What? What do you mean? It's your ranch."

"No, son. Not anymore. We have no desire to go back there. We love traveling and if we settle down, it's going to be somewhere a lot warmer than Montana in the winter," Brody's dad told him.

"I'd take great care of it," Brody promised.

"We know you would but you would have to stay. No running off again," his mother scolded.

Brody clenched his jaw. "I didn't 'run off' mom. I joined the Marshals."

"Yes, but you left the girl you loved behind. You need to settle down, Brody and if you want the ranch, it's yours but only if you agree to stay. Promise."

Brody hesitated. Could he stay? He'd always loved working the ranch until he got older, then he'd wanted out of Clifton but now, he had a chance to have the ranch and make it work. "I promise mom, dad. Of course, I'll stay and take care of it."

They continued to talk about the ranch and sending him the deed for it and then hung up. Brody still couldn't believe they'd given him the ranch. It was actually his now and he was looking forward to buying some Angus. He'd wait until he could get a weekend off, then he'd go to an auction and buy his cattle.

Brody stood and headed down the hallway. He stopped at all five bedrooms to take sheets off the furniture and open windows. The entire house had cherry hardwood floors, which all needed to be cleaned, but he'd get to it. Entering his parents' old room, he stripped the bed and put clean sheets on. This would be his room now. It was a large room with a row of windows on one wall, a closet opposite and a fireplace beside a door, which led to a large bathroom. Pushing the door open, he entered the room and glanced around. The bathtub and shower only needed wiped out so he went about cleaning them so he could shower and get some sleep before starting work tomorrow night. He shook his head, he

Brody
21

hated night shift.

Chapter Two

The next night, Brody was working with Mark Shaw. They drove through the streets of town and headed for Dewey's bar.

"We check Dewey's out every night," Mark told him. "It can get a little rowdy, especially on a Friday night." They drove through the parking lot. "It looks like it's packed tonight."

"Do we go in or just cruise around?" Brody asked.

Mark glanced over and grinned. "We go in. Odds are someone's pissed at someone else."

Brody grumbled. "You're probably right."

Mark parked the cruiser and they strolled inside. The place was wall-to-wall people. Brody and Mark weaved their way through the crowd. No one seemed to care about them being there. Mark signaled for Brody to head in the opposite direction. Brody nodded and made his way through the crowd. He came to a halt when a woman stepped in front of him.

"Brody Morgan." The raven-haired beauty smiled up at him. He drew a blank.

He grinned. "You have me at a disadvantage."

"Brianna Porter." She grinned at him.

"Brianna? Tom's little sister?" His gaze roamed down over her.

Brianna laughed. "Yes. It's me. I've grown up. The last time you saw me, I was sixteen."

Brody grinned. "Well, you've certainly gotten more beautiful."

Brody

Brianna laughed as she rubbed her hand up and down his arm. "And you've gotten more gorgeous."

Brody chuckled. "I'm working, hon."

She poked her bottom lip out. "What time do you...get off?"

Brody almost groaned. It had been a while since he'd had sex and she was clearly offering. "Seven tomorrow morning."

Brianna shrugged. "Want my number? I wouldn't mind if you stopped by on your way home tomorrow morning."

Brody started to answer her when a fight broke out. After giving her an apologetic grin, he headed toward the fight. Mark got there at the same time. Brody grabbed one of the men and Mark grabbed the other. They pulled them apart. One of them swung at Brody, clipping his shoulder. Brody slammed the man down on the table and handcuffed him then pulled him up and read him his rights. The other man punched Mark in the face, making Mark let go. The man then pulled a knife. Everyone jumped back.

"Put the knife away, Carl," Mark insisted as he rubbed his sore jaw.

"So you can take me to jail? I don't think so Shaw," Carl slurred.

"You're going to jail any way you put it." Mark grinned.

Carl swung the knife in a wide arc. Brody pushed the man he had handcuffed down into a chair and leaned over him. "Do not move. You understand?" The man nodded. Brody moved to the side of Carl. Opposite of Mark.

Brody

24

"Put the knife down, Carl," Brody quietly said.

"Brody? What the hell are you doing here?" Carl slurred his words.

"I'm a deputy now and we're going to take you and your friend in."

Carl laughed. "Mr. Big Shot U S Marshal is a *deputy* now. That's rich."

Brody flattened his lips into a thin line and clenched his jaw. "I'm still an officer of the law and I can either take you in or shoot you." He shrugged. "It doesn't matter to me which it is."

Carl's eyes widened as he glanced at Mark, who grinned at him. "I'm with Brody on this one."

Brody could see the fight going out of Carl and as soon as he had the chance, Brody jumped him. Mark charged at Carl, too. They both took him down. When they stood up with him, the crowd cheered. Brody and Mark shook their heads. Mark took care of Carl while Brody lifted the other man from the chair.

"My wife's gonna kill me," the man muttered.

As Brody was hauling him toward the door, Brianna stepped in front of him and put a slip of paper in his pocket.

"Call me. I don't care what time it is." She smiled at him.

Brody nodded and moved out the door and shoved the man into the back of the cruiser and got into the front seat. He took a deep breath and let it out. Mark got in and they rode to the Sheriff's department. The two men in the back seat sat silent.

* * * *

Madilyn was a wreck. Since seeing Brody

yesterday, she was literally a wreck. Tears threatened to fall and it was taking everything she had not to let them. Why had he come back? After leaving her to work in Butte, why had he come back? She put her hands over her face and let the tears fall. How was she going to be in the same town with him? Was he staying or was it just a stop on his way to somewhere else? Madilyn jerked when her phone rang. Picking it up, she mentally groaned when she heard Zach's voice.

"How about dinner later, Madilyn?" Zach Johnson asked.

Madilyn wanted to say no but she liked Zach and he was a nice man, a man in love with her, wanted to marry her, and knew all about her past with Brody.

"That sounds nice." She tried to sound enthused but she didn't fool him.

Zach sighed. "You know he's back, don't you?"

"Yes...I'm fine, Zach. I'd love to go to dinner with you."

"I'll pick you up at seven. No need to dress up, we'll just hit the diner."

Madilyn agreed and disconnected the call. Would she ever get to the point where she'd love another man? Would another man ever make her forget Brody? She and Zach had been dating for almost a year but she wasn't in love with him. She hadn't been able to bring herself to go to bed with him. He didn't pressure her, but she knew he wanted to take her to bed. He wanted sex and it amazed Madilyn he kept waiting on her. She couldn't do it. She hadn't had sex with anyone since Brody, and Zach deserved so much better. A woman to love him, not to use him as a substitute for a man she couldn't have. There was no doubt in Madilyn's mind, if she let Brody know she wanted him he'd be there, but she didn't want to fall into his trap again. Her heart couldn't take it again. Unless he was involved with someone. Oh, God. She'd never thought of that. Just because he was back didn't mean he didn't have someone in his life. What if he's married now? His wife could be at the ranch. He could have children. *Stop it!* Madilyn stood and headed for the shower. Zach would be there in two hours. The shop closed at noon on Saturdays and wasn't open at all on Sunday. Katie liked spending time with her husband on the weekends, although if the rumors were true, Kevin Parker wasn't home much, he had a mistress he'd rather be with. Madilyn couldn't understand why Katie put up with his indiscretions but it really wasn't any of her business. The two women had become great friends over the years they'd worked together but Katie didn't mention her husband much and Madilyn couldn't bring herself to ask.

Madilyn wanted a husband, a good man to treat her like a queen, but he'd left her years ago. In her heart, she knew Brody would never cheat on her. He loved her. At one time, he'd loved her with all his heart. Her throat tightened and more tears threatened. *Damn it!* She'd been fine until she found out he was back and then seeing him nearly brought her to her knees. God, she so wanted to just curl into a ball and wish the world

Brody

away. At least, wish Brody Morgan away. He looked so good. His dark eyes could talk her in or out of anything. The night he'd gazed into her eyes and talked her out of her clothes was proof of that. They'd been going together only six months when it happened. At nineteen, she'd given him her virginity and her heart and soul.

Shaking away the memories, she stepped from the shower, grabbed a fluffy pink towel, and dried off. Going out to dinner was the last thing she wanted to do. The temptation to cancel was strong but it wasn't fair to Zach. Sighing, Madilyn strolled into her bedroom and dressed. The light green summer dress matched her eyes. She applied light make-up and slid her feet into green wedge sandals. The three inch wedge heels put her just under five eleven. Zach stood at five eleven. Madilyn never wore higher heels when she was going out with him. She'd never had a problem with Brody since he topped six four. *Stop thinking about him!* Madilyn blinked quickly to keep the tears back. Huffing, she took a seat on the sofa and waited for Zach to arrive.

* * * *

Brody and Mark sat at the counter of the diner eating dinner. His shift had just started, and not much was going on in the town. Brody was fine with that after the trouble at Dewey's bar last night. The bell over the diner rang and he instinctively glanced in that direction. He was sure his mouth fell open as he watched Madilyn walk in with Zach Johnson behind her. It was evident they were together. Brody flattened his mouth into a thin line as he glared at them. He knew the instant she spotted him; she faltered in her steps but moved her gaze away from his. Brody swung his gaze to Zach and saw him smirk. *Son of a bitch!* What the hell was she doing with Johnson?

"They've been dating a while," Mark muttered.

Brody whipped his head toward him. "What?"

Mark shrugged. "You asked what she was doing with him."

Shit! Brody hadn't realized he'd spoken the words aloud. "How long is a while?"

Mark rubbed his chin. "Close to a year, I believe."

Brody clenched his jaw as he swung his gaze back to the woman he'd always love. No matter how many he'd been with in the past five years, Madilyn was the only one he wanted. Now she was dating Zach and had been for almost a year. Zach's hand was on her lower back and Brody wanted to snap it like a twig. In all likelihood, she was sleeping with Zach. Brody's fist tightened around his coffee cup so hard he was surprised it didn't shatter.

"Don't break my cup, Brody," Connie, the owner of the diner, scolded him.

He loosened his grip but still clenched his jaw as he watched them sit in a booth. Madilyn sat with her back to him. Zach stared at him. Brody raised an eyebrow at him. They'd never gotten along. Zach had been a year ahead of him in school. The school jock. Quarterback of the football team. Blond hair with blue eyes. Brody kicked his ass once and Zach never got over it. Brody knew Zach was enjoying himself.

Brody

* * * *

"Are you all right with him being here?" Zach asked her.

"I'm fine. It just took me by surprise when we first came in." Madilyn shrugged. "I have to get used to seeing him for as long as he's here."

"As long as he's here? You think he's going to leave again?"

"It's what he does."

"I sure as hell hope he does," Zach muttered.

Madilyn glared at him. "I guess we'll see, won't we?"

"I'm sorry. I'm just thinking of you." Zach smiled at her.

Madilyn scoffed. "Sure."

Connie took their orders and moved away. Madilyn knew it wouldn't matter what she ordered. It would taste like sawdust. Zach was jealous of Brody. He always had been. Madilyn was aware of their history. Everyone in Clifton was. The high school quarterback didn't make it to college. His dream of going pro fell apart when his parents divorced before he graduated from high school. Zach started selling real estate and although he made a good living at it, he was in no way near as wealthy as Brody's family. Brody's parents had, at one time, the most lucrative beef ranch in northern Montana. They'd made more than enough money to retire on and travel. The house sat empty for the past two years and they sold off all the Angus. Madilyn wanted to look over her shoulder at him but knew she couldn't. Taking a deep breath, she picked up her tea and drank. Her gaze moved to

Zach when he snorted.

"What was that for?" she asked.

"He's dying to come back here."

"What makes you think so?"

Zach glanced at her. "He keeps looking back here. I wish he would."

Madilyn snickered and then sobered when Zach glared at her. She shrugged. There was no way Zach would win in a fight against Brody. For one thing, Zach wasn't in as good of shape as she was sure Brody was. Brody always kept in shape by working out. His body was hard. He had to keep in shape being a Marshal and she couldn't see him letting himself go. Zach, on the other hand, was soft. He didn't work out and although he wasn't fat, he didn't have the body or muscle Brody did.

"You're still in love with him," Zach sneered.

Madilyn gasped. "I will *not* discuss Brody with you or anyone else for that matter." She set her tea down, slid out of the booth, and strode from the restaurant. She heard Connie yelling at Zach as she went out the door.

"You need to pay for your dinners, Zach. Whether you ate them or not."

* * * *

Brody watched as Madilyn left the restaurant and Zach halt when Connie called out to him. Zach tried to dig his wallet out, all the while gazing out the door to where Madilyn marched down the sidewalk. Zach seemed to be all fingers.

Brody spun around on his stool and stood. He nodded his head at Zach and moved out the door. He spotted Madilyn a block ahead and ran after her, catching her before she crossed the street.

"Problem with your date?"

Madilyn spun around and narrowed her eyes at him. "Go away." She crossed the street.

Brody chuckled and trotted behind her. When she spun around, he almost ran into her.

"I mean it Brody Thomas Morgan. Leave. Me. Alone."

"Shit, using the middle name. That's cold, Maddie." He drew back when she slapped her hand at him.

"Don't call me that." Her jaw clenched.

"Sorry," Brody muttered then swore when he saw Zach running toward them. "Here comes your boyfriend."

Madilyn growled. "He's not my boyfriend."

Brody raised his eyebrows. "You've been seeing him for almost a year and he's not your boyfriend?"

"How do you know how long I've been seeing him?" Madilyn placed her hands on her hips and narrowed her eyes at him.

He grinned. "I asked."

"You..." Her jaw went slack.

Zach stopped beside Madilyn. "Is he bothering you?"

Brody grunted. "What if I am?" He folded his arms across his chest. "What are you planning on doing about it, Johnson?"

Zach stepped forward but when Brody didn't budge, he halted in his tracks. "You'd love it if I took a swing, wouldn't you? You'd arrest me."

Brody glanced at Zach. "We can finish this

when I get off duty." He raised an eyebrow. While Brody and Zach stared at each other, Madilyn swore softly and walked away.

"Your...date's leaving." Brody sneered and then chuckled when Zach ran off after her.

Zach stopped and spun around and glared at him. "I won't have you hurting her again."

"What happens between Madilyn and me is our business, not yours." Brody stepped toward him. He smirked when Zach backed up a step.

"I'm not afraid of you, Morgan."

Brody smiled. "Yes you are."

Zach glared at him before he turned and ran after Madilyn. Brody folded his arms across his chest and stared after them.

* * * *

Madilyn unlocked her apartment door just as Zach got to her. When he touched her arm, she spun around and glared at him.

"Go away, Zach."

"Come on, Madilyn. It isn't my fault," Zach pleaded.

"Seriously? You were the one saying I'm still in love with Brody." Madilyn clenched her jaw.

Zach sighed. "You're right, and I'm sorry. Let me come in, and I'll make it up to you."

No way in hell! ran through her mind. Going to bed with him was not going to happen. Especially after seeing Brody in his khaki deputy shirt with his badge pinned to it and the short sleeves tight around his biceps. He wore jeans and the way he filled them out made her bite the inside of her cheek to hold back a groan. She knew every inch of his hard body and loved it.

Even the tattoos he had under his shirt. Madilyn wondered if he'd had her name removed. It was across the top of his left pec, in cursive. She'd loved it when he showed it to her and she never got the chance to reveal his name she'd had tattooed on the front of her right hip.

"No. I'm done. I can't go out with you anymore. Throwing Brody in my face shows me how you really feel." She started to push the door shut when he stuck his foot in it. "Go away, Zach."

"I don't think so." He shoved the door open and wrapped his fingers around her arm. "I really don't care if you're still in love with him or not. I've had it with all the sexual frustration you put me through the past year."

"Let go of me," she shouted.

Zach jerked her to him and tried to kiss her. She kicked his shin and screamed.

"I think she wants you to let go of her."

Madilyn gasped as she spun around to see Brody leaning against the doorjamb with his arms folded across his broad chest. Her gaze swept down his body, lingering on the worn fly of his jeans, where they emphasized his sex, and down to his worn boots. Her eyes traveled back up to land on his gorgeous face, but Brody wasn't looking at her. His gaze was trained on Zach and she'd seen him mad enough times to know he was furious.

Zach stared at him with his fingers still wrapped around her bicep. She watched as Brody's gaze moved to Zach's hand and back to his face. "Remove your hand, or I'll remove it for you. Now," he said with deadly calm as he pushed himself away from the door and stared at Zach. Madilyn could see a muscle in his jaw twitching, a sure sign he was on the edge.

Zach let go of her. "This is none of your business, Morgan."

"I'm a sheriff's deputy of course it's my business. Do you want to press charges?" He turned his gaze to her and raised an eyebrow. She shook her head. "Leave." Brody jerked his head toward the door behind him.

Zach started toward the door but Brody didn't move, making Zach step around him. When he was even with him, Brody growled. "Touch her again and we'll finish this." When Zach started to walk past, Brody gripped his arm. "We clear on that?" Zach nodded and Brody gave him a shove.

Madilyn let out a breath when Zach stormed out. Brody pushed the door closed.

"Are you all right?" he asked.

Madilyn nodded. "Thank you. He..." She shrugged. "He wouldn't leave."

"I heard. I'm glad I decided to follow you."

"Why did you?" Madilyn folded her arms.

Brody shrugged. "I didn't like the look in his eyes after you took off. Call it a cop's intuition."

Madilyn tilted her head. "I'm glad you trusted your gut." She shivered.

Brody stepped toward her and ran his hands up and down her arms. Madilyn gazed up into his brown eyes and smiled.

"Still wearing the glasses, huh?"

Brody grumbled. "I went through this with Sam. I can't stand to put anything in my eyes."

He shrugged. "I'll always have to wear them and the older I get, the more I'll have to."

Their eyes held. His hands ran up to her shoulders, to her neck and into her hair. Madilyn moaned. Brody lowered his head and pressed his lips to hers. Her arms circled around his waist. Brody pulled her tight against him, and took her mouth in a deep kiss. His mouth moved across her cheek to her ear. Taking the lobe between his teeth, he sucked it into his mouth, making her shiver.

"Brody..." she moaned when his lips came back to hers.

"I want you, Madilyn. I've missed you so much," he whispered against her lips before sliding his tongue between them.

She pulled away. "Don't...please."

"What is it? You want me, I know you do." He ran his tongue along her neck and then inhaled deeply. "God, you smell fantastic. You always did."

"Brody..." His mouth interrupted her. She pushed at his shoulders, making him pull back. "I can't do this. Not now. Not ever."

Brody stepped back. "You're not going to let it go, are you?"

Madilyn shook her head. "Did you think I was joking when you left? I said I'd never forgive you. I've moved on."

"By sleeping with Johnson?" Brody growled.

"That is none of your business," she shouted. "Tell me you haven't slept with anyone since you left."

Brody glanced away from her and back.

Brody

"You're right, I'm sorry."

Madilyn huffed. "That's what I thought. You can go now."

Brody gave her a brisk nod and walked out, leaving Madilyn staring at the door.

Chapter Three

The next morning, Brody was in the office filling out his work sheet when Sam walked in.

"How's it going?" Sam asked.

"Good." Brody didn't look up as he filled out the form. He glanced up when Sam didn't move. "What?"

"It's all over town you ran out of the diner to chase Madilyn." Sam grinned.

"Jesus Christ!" Brody took off his glasses and tossed them on the desk then he ran his hand down his face. "I shouldn't be surprised."

Sam chuckled. "No, you shouldn't. So what was that all about?" He leaned his hip against the table.

"I wanted to find out why she stormed out on Johnson."

Sam snorted. "I don't know what she sees in him. I never did like him."

"Hell, you know I never got along with him. They came into the diner and were having dinner when she got up and stormed out." Brody shrugged. "I wanted to know why."

"Brody..."

"I know, Sam. I know. She's still so beautiful...I just," He sighed. "I don't know."

"Christ," Sam muttered. "Don't hurt her again. You didn't see what you did to her when you left her."

"I asked her to go with me. She refused." Brody stood and glared at Sam.

Brody

"You know why she refused. Hell Brody, she'd just buried her father."

"Tell me this, Sam. What would you have done?"

"I don't know." Sam shook his head. "I honestly don't know."

Brody nodded. "Right. It was what I wanted to do with my life at the time."

"At the time. We need to talk about that." Sam narrowed his eyes. "I want to know why you left the Marshals."

"Suffice it to say, I burned out." Brody handed Sam the paperwork.

"You know all I have to do is make a phone call?"

"I know, but I'm hoping you'll give me some time." Brody shook his head. "I'll tell you what happened. Just give me time."

Sam nodded. "You got it. Go home and get some rest. I'll see you tomorrow."

Brody hesitated, and then nodded. He strode from the office, hopped on his bike, and glanced toward Madilyn's apartment complex. Sighing, he started the bike and pulled out of the lot, heading home. He was tired. Damn nightshift about killed him. The bike wound down the curved road and knolls as he headed home. Going around the turn known as 'Dead Man's Curve' he moved closer to the right. It wasn't close enough. A truck came around the curve on the wrong side and it took every bit of Brody's power to keep the bike upright but when it hit the gravel, he lost it and the bike flipped. Brody hit the ditch and rolled several times. He laid there stunned and tried to catch his breath. The truck kept going.

When he tried to stand, he couldn't. He tried to take deep breaths. He'd bet his last dollar he had a few cracked or broken ribs. Pulling out his cell phone, he called Sam as he lay flat on his back in the ditch.

"Some jerk in a truck just ran me off the road," Brody told Sam when he answered.

"Are you all right?"

"I think I might have some cracked ribs. Son of a bitch kept going but I saw the truck enough to give you a description." Brody couldn't breathe without feeling pain.

"Tell me," Sam demanded. He swore when Brody described it.

"You know who it is?" Brody asked.

"Sounds like Joe Baker. He's always drunk. I'll send Rick out to his place. Do you need an ambulance and a tow truck?"

"Yes to both. I think the bike's totaled and I know I need to see a doctor. Why the hell is the guy drunk at seven thirty in the morning?" Brody sighed.

"Where are you?" Sam asked.

"Copper Ridge. Dead Man's Curve," Brody whispered, trying not to breathe.

"It probably was Baker. He lives out that way and he's never sober. I'll be right there."

Brody hung up and tried to move to a sitting position but he couldn't. He continued to lay there as he waited for Sam. As he glanced over to the bike, he swore. Looked like he was buying a truck sooner than he'd expected. He heard the sirens and sighed then hissed in a breath at the pain.

An hour later, Brody was still sitting in the hospital room waiting for the doctor to come in. This is why he hated going to a hospital. The waiting. Sighing, he laid his hand over his ribs. Damn it hurt to breathe. Brody was about to slide off the table when a nurse stepped in the room, pushing a wheelchair.

"Mister Morgan? We need to take you to x-ray to check your ribs." She glanced up at him and smiled. Brody tried to smile but his ribs were killing him. The nurse moved forward to help him. He tried not to breathe as he sat in the chair. "I'm sorry you're in pain but we can't prescribe anything until we see exactly what's wrong."

"My ribs are cracked, that's what's wrong," Brody swore. "It's not the first time and it probably won't be the last."

"I see," she murmured as she wheeled him down the hall to x-ray. Sam stopped them in the hall.

"I'll be in the waiting room and then I'll drive you home. You'll need to take a few days off."

"Hell no, Sam. I don't need any days off," Brody argued.

"I said you're taking some days off. I'm your boss." Sam glared at him.

Brody took a deep breath and almost passed out from the pain. "All right." Not that he wanted to, but he knew with the pain he was in he'd be no help at all to Mark. His ribs would heal in a few days if he rested. But he knew he could at

Brody

least go into the office to help.

"I can help in the office," Brody suggested.

Sam shook his head. "No. You will stay home and heal." He glanced at the nurse. "How long could he be out for?"

"Usually six weeks to heal if they're fractured. We'll know more after the x-rays." She smiled up at Sam.

Brody noticed they kept staring at each other so he coughed and regretted it the minute he did it. Sam whipped his head around. "Are you all right?"

Brody glared up at him until Sam grinned at him. "I'll be in the waiting room." He put his fingers to his hat, smiled at the nurse and walked off. The nurse began pushing the wheelchair down the hall again. Brody kept his hand against his ribcage. He jumped and then groaned at the pain when the nurse ran the wheelchair into the doorway. Brody glanced back at her.

"I'm so sorry. I was…" Her cheeks turned pink.

"He's not married, if you want to know," Brody growled. Sam never had trouble getting women. It had always been a pissing contest between himself, Riley Madison, Ryder Wolfe, Jake, Gabe, and Wyatt Stone, Trick Dillon, and Sam when it came to females, but the only one he was ever interested in was Madilyn.

"He's not?" She sighed. "He's gorgeous."

"Yeah, whatever." Brody muttered. He was a good-looking man himself and he had plenty of women after him, as long as Garrett wasn't around. Brody grunted. It never mattered to him

Brody

after he'd found Madilyn. Sam could have all the women he wanted, Brody wanted Madilyn and no one else, and he'd royally fucked that up. The nurse didn't say anymore as she wheeled him into the room. The x-ray technician helped Brody up onto the table. After the nurse told him she'd be back for him, she left.

"We need to take your shirt off, hon. I'm sorry but it's going to hurt like hell," the technician told him. She helped him remove his shirt and stared at his tattoos. "I love a man with tats."

Brody tried to smile but he was in too much pain to muster one up for her. She helped him lie back and then left the room. She told him to hold his breath while she took the pictures. After a few minutes, she came out and helped him put his shirt back on. She grinned at him.

"Is Madilyn your woman?"

Brody glanced down to his left pec. "She used to be."

"Well, if she were smart, she'd take you back." She winked at him.

Brody laughed and groaned at the pain. Shaking his head, he told her. "I don't see that happening."

The technician laughed. "That's too bad. I'm Nancy, by the way. Call me." She stuck a card into his shirt pocket and left to call the nurse to come back and get him. Brody smiled.

* * * *

Madilyn sat up when she heard the siren go by and then ran to the window and watched as Sam's SUV cruiser drove past. He was heading out toward Copper Ridge Road. Too many accidents happened on the winding road. Madilyn hoped it wasn't anyone she knew. She heard a second siren and knew it was an ambulance, which was never a good sign. It meant someone was hurt. It was a boring evening. Zach had called her several times but she refused to speak with him. He tried apologizing but what he'd done was unforgivable. It could've gotten way out of hand if Brody hadn't shown up. She shivered thinking what might have happened. Maybe she should've pressed charges. Was it possible Zach would do that to another woman?

Madilyn blew out a breath. She should have told Brody she wanted to press charges. Zach had scared her immensely. When someone knocked on her door, she flinched. Going to the peephole, she peered through it and saw Zach. What did he think he was doing?

"I know you're in there, Madilyn. Come on, open up so we can talk," Zach's voice came through the door.

"No. Go away or I'll call Sam."

"You don't really want to do that. I'm sorry. I just want to apologize."

"You just did, now go," Madilyn told him.

"Let me say it to your face, Madilyn. Please."

"Go away, Zach, or I'm calling Sam," she repeated. Madilyn heard him swear and then a loud thump hit against the door, as if he'd struck it with his fist.

"This isn't over. I'll be back," Zach shouted.

Madilyn backed away from the door, staring at it. Now he was scaring her. Should she call

Sam? Picking up her phone, she called the Sheriff's Department. She knew Sam was out but maybe Rick could come over. Betty Lou transferred her.

"Sheriff Garrett," Sam answered.

"Sam? I thought Betty Lou was going to transfer me to Rick. It's Madilyn."

"He's all right, Madilyn. He just has some busted ribs."

"Who? Rick?" She was confused.

"Rick? No. Brody," Sam told her.

Madilyn gasped. "Brody's hurt?"

Sam swore. "Joe Baker ran him off the road and he flipped the bike. The nurse took him down to x-ray to see if his ribs are broken or bruised. Brody's sure there are a few broken."

"I'm on my way." Madilyn hung up before Sam had a chance to answer her. She had to get to Brody. He was hurt. The tears in her eyes were blinding her as she ran out to her car. Tearing out of the parking lot, she headed for the hospital, going well over the speed limit. She pulled into the hospital parking lot, found a spot, and ran inside. She didn't see Sam anywhere so she walked to the desk. "I'm looking for Brody Morgan," Madilyn told the nurse sitting behind the counter. She watched as the nurse scanned her computer.

"He's back in E R room fifteen. Are you family?"

"I..." Madilyn didn't know what to say.

"Madilyn." She spun around when she heard Sam's voice.

"Sam. Is he all right?"

Brody

"I told you he was on the phone. You didn't need to come here," Sam scolded her.

"I have to see him, Sam. Please." Madilyn hated the catch in her voice.

Sam wrapped his arm around her shoulder and led her to the room. Neither of them saw the nurse give them a dirty look. Madilyn let Sam lead her into the room. Her breath whooshed out when she saw Brody sitting up on the bed. He frowned at her.

"Madilyn? What are you doing here?" He turned his gaze to Sam. "Did you call her?"

"No." Sam looked at her. "Why were you calling the department anyway if you didn't know about the wreck?"

Madilyn nibbled on her bottom lip. There was no way she was going to tell them about Zach scaring her. Knowing Brody as well as she did, she knew he'd go after Zach, busted ribs and all. She shook her head. "It doesn't matter now." She turned to Brody. "Are your ribs broken?"

Brody shook his head. "Two of them are cracked, none are broken."

Madilyn nodded not knowing what to do now that she was there. "I'll, uh...go then."

"Madilyn," Brody whispered.

"What?" She looked everywhere but at him. She noticed Sam slip out of the room.

"You were worried about me?" Brody grinned when she shook her head. "Yes you were. Why else are you here?"

Madilyn huffed. "You'll never get me to admit it." Folding her arms across her chest, she glared at him.

Brody

Brody chuckled then sucked in a breath. "Son of a bitch."

Madilyn was at his side in no time. "Are you all right?"

"No. It hurts like a motherfu...uh, like a bitch."

The nurse entered the room and handed Brody a release paper to sign and two prescriptions.

"Make sure you follow the directions. No lifting anything until the ribs heal. The doctor wants you to see your primary care physician before returning to work. Take the pain meds as needed and you *will* need them. They're very strong. Do you have someone who can stay with you or check on you?" She glanced toward Madilyn.

Madilyn shook her head. "No."

"I'll be fine," Brody assured the nurse.

"Make sure you are. You can't take a chance of hurting yourself any worse."

Brody gave a nod and slowly got down from the bed. He clenched his teeth as he straightened up. The nurse nodded toward the wheelchair.

"I can walk out," Brody muttered.

"You're going out in the wheelchair. Hospital policy." The nurse glared at him until she saw Sam come into the room. She smiled up at him. Madilyn noticed one corner of Sam's mouth lift, and then he looked toward Brody.

"Are you giving her a rough time?" Sam nodded toward the nurse.

"I don't want to ride out in a wheelchair. It hurts too much to lower myself down into it and then to get up." Brody shook his head. "No. I'm walking out. What are they going to do about it?" He slowly walked out the door. Madilyn, Sam, and the nurse stared after him.

Madilyn drove home wiping tears from her cheeks. Damn him for getting hurt. Shaking her head, she knew it was wrong to think that way. It wasn't Brody's fault Joe Baker was drunk again and ran him off the road. God, he could've been killed. Madilyn's tears rolled down her cheeks. She was never going to stop loving him. Never. Loving him was as much a part of her as breathing was. Brody Morgan would always have her heart. She slapped the steering wheel. Damn him. Why couldn't he have stayed away? Why was he back? Not to become a deputy, she knew that. Something was up. He'd been a U S Marshal for five years and now, all of a sudden, he's a deputy in a small town Sheriff's office? Madilyn shook her head. It made no sense. As she pulled into her parking space, she saw Zach standing by the stairs to her apartment and she was terrified. What part of go away did he not understand?

Madilyn took a deep breath and called Sam. After a quick explanation, she hung up and stayed in the car. She saw Zach frown as he practically marched toward her. She lowered the window a few inches.

"Go away, Zach."

He leaned his arms atop the car and stared down at her. "Come on, Madilyn. This is getting ridiculous. I just want to apologize."

"You have. Several times. We're done talking. Go. Away," Madilyn said through clenched teeth.

Zach tried to open her car door and finding it locked made him angry. "Get out of the car, Madilyn, and we'll go inside and talk." He slapped his hand on top of the car.

Madilyn was about to yell at him when Sam's sport utility cruiser pulled up. She watched as Sam stepped out of the vehicle and slowly walked toward her car. She heard Zach hiss in a breath.

"You called the sheriff?" he growled.

Madilyn watched as Sam leaned against the front of his vehicle, folded his arms, and crossed his booted ankles. She couldn't see his eyes behind his aviator sunglasses but she was sure he was glaring at Zach.

"What are you doing, Zach?" Sam asked as he tilted his head.

"Nothing. We're just talking." Zach straightened up.

Madilyn watched as Sam glanced away and then back to Zach. She pushed her door open and got out. "I've asked him to leave but he won't."

Zach spun around to face her. His eyed narrowed. "I just wanted to say I was sorry."

"Sorry for what?" Sam moved closer.

"I don't think it's any of your business...Sheriff," Zach told him.

Madilyn looked up at Sam. "You can ask Brody about it. I didn't press charges but if Zach doesn't leave me alone, I will."

"You bitch," Zach said through clenched teeth as he moved toward her.

"That's enough," Sam didn't raise his voice but he may as well have. Zach froze in his tracks. "Do you want to file a restraining order Madilyn?"

Madilyn huffed. "No." She glanced at Zach. "Not yet. I just want him to leave me alone. It's over."

"Madilyn—" Zach started.

"You heard her. It's over. Move on, Zach," Sam interrupted. "Get in your car and go home. Don't make me arrest you for harassment."

Madilyn watched as Zach wrestled with himself. She could see he wasn't happy but he gave Sam a nod and after glaring at Madilyn one last time, he moved toward his car. She let out the breath she'd been holding.

"Are you all right?" Sam touched her shoulder.

She nodded. "Yes. Thank you for getting here so fast."

Sam shrugged. "I was on my way back from taking Brody home. I was almost here when you called."

"How is Brody?"

"Hurting. He will be for a while. I made sure he took a pain pill and laid down before I left." Sam shook his head. "I don't know how he's going to take care of himself, he can barely get around."

"I could check on him." *What?* Where had that come from? Madilyn started to shake her head.

"That'd be great. He needs someone to check on him for a few weeks until he can get around better. I just don't have the time. With him being out, I'm going to have to move everyone around. I like having two deputies together at all times, and I can't do it with Brody out."

Madilyn nodded. Now what? She couldn't do

it. There was no way she could go out to the ranch and help Brody. Too many things had happened between them at the ranch. Too many memories. How many times had they spent the night in his room when his parents were out of town? How many times had they made love in the hayloft? Shaking her head, she gazed up at Sam and saw him staring at her.

"If you don't want to do it, Madilyn, I'll figure something out," Sam told her.

Great! She took a deep breath. "I'm fine with it, Sam." *Liar!* Why couldn't she just say she couldn't do it? Because it would put more on Sam and with a deputy out, he had enough on his hands. She smiled up at him. "I can do it."

Sam grinned at her. "I appreciate it. You'll need to go out there later today and tomorrow morning to check on him. Knowing Brody, he'll be up and trying to do something and not take those pills. Whether he wants to admit it or not, he needs those pain meds every eight hours."

"I'll go later this afternoon and first thing tomorrow." She turned away and then back. "Thank you for coming over. Zach was scaring me."

"Let me know if you have any other problems with him. I won't mind hauling his ass in if I have to." Sam narrowed his eyes. "I never liked him."

Madilyn cleared her throat. "I know. I really don't know why I dated him for so long."

"Well, as I said, let me know if you have any more run-ins with him. Have a good day." Sam sauntered back to his cruiser and drove off.

Madilyn groaned. *What were you thinking? I*

Brody

could check on him...you're just asking for trouble here, Madilyn girl. Nothing but trouble.

Sighing, she entered her apartment. The shop wasn't open since it was Sunday and it was the day of the week she cleaned her apartment and washed clothes. Now she had to add in going to check on Brody. Madilyn chewed on her bottom lip. How was she going to do this? Taking a deep breath, she started her laundry and tidied up. The hours seemed to fly by. It seemed like it was no time at all that she was driving out to the ranch to check on Brody. She groaned. She seriously did not want to do this. Madilyn pulled around to the back of the house. She knocked on the back door then pushed it open.

"Brody?" she called out and walked toward the living room. She came to a dead stop when she saw him lying on the couch asleep. He didn't have a shirt on and though his jeans were zipped, they were unsnapped. Leaning over, she saw he still had the tattoo of her name across the top of his bicep. The fact she was here confirmed he wasn't in a relationship of any kind. Her gaze roamed over his hard body. He still kept in shape there was no question there. His pecs were solid muscle. A tattoo twisted around each bicep. Her eyes ran down the six-pack stomach and back up. She gasped when she saw his eyes were open.

"What are you doing here, Madilyn?" he asked in a low voice.

She cleared her throat. "Uh, we want to make sure you take your meds."

"We?" Brody moved to sit up but winced.

Brody

Madilyn moved forward to help him but stopped at the look he gave her. "I can do it," he growled. "And who's *we*?"

"Fine." She sighed. "Sam and me. We both know how stubborn you are."

Brody leaned back against the couch once he sat up. His hand moved over his ribs. "Christ that hurt," he muttered.

"It's time for your meds."

"I don't need…" He moaned when he tried to get up.

"The hell you don't," Madilyn shouted. "You will take the meds if I have to ram them down your throat, Brody Thomas Morgan."

"*Shit!* Middle name again," he mumbled as he glanced up at her.

Madilyn tried not to grin but she couldn't help herself. "You knew you were in trouble anytime your mom yelled it."

"Yeah, and then you started doing it." Brody leaned his head back. "I couldn't win with you two."

"How are your parents, Brody?" Madilyn took a seat in the chair across from him.

"Having a ball traveling. They call me every week to tell me where they're heading next. I'm glad they're enjoying their retirement."

"Me too. I loved your parents." Madilyn smiled.

"They loved you too." Brody's eyes met hers. "Almost as much as I did."

Madilyn tore her eyes from his and stood. "I'll get you some water."

* * * *

Brody watched as she walked past him. He

couldn't help saying it. He had loved her. He *did* love her. She'd never take him back, he knew it with all his heart. Madilyn hated him because he left her. Not only that but he was still in law enforcement. Madilyn didn't want a law man. She wanted 'safe' and Brody wasn't it. He closed his eyes, listening to her in the kitchen getting a glass, ice, and then water. When she cleared her throat, Brody slowly opened his eyes and gazed up at her. His heart stopped. He loved her so much.

"Your water." Madilyn shoved the glass toward him.

"Thanks." Brody took it from her, noticing she did everything not to touch him. He raised an eyebrow at her and saw her cheeks turn pink.

"Is it that hard, Madilyn?"

"Is what that hard?"

"Being around me."

"Yes. I don't want to be around you at all, but I told Sam I'd do this. So, take your pill so I can leave."

Brody ran his hand over his mouth as his jaw clenched. "Then don't do it! I don't need you to nurse me. I can take care of myself." He picked up the pill, threw it into his mouth and drank his water then slammed the empty glass on the table. He glared up at her. "Go. Get out and don't bother coming back." He heard her gasp. When she placed her hand over her mouth, he felt like an ass. "Madilyn..."

She shook her head and ran from the room. Brody swore and tried to stand. The pain was excruciating and he slumped down onto the couch. The back door slammed and then her car started up and he heard her driving away. *Way to go, Morgan. You just ran off the woman you love for the second time in your life. Dumbass!* Brody slowly lay down, placed his forearm over his eyes, and turned the air blue as he swore, thinking of how he'd hurt her. Again.

Chapter Four

Four weeks later Brody was going insane. He called Sam to ask him if he'd take Brody to a dealership to purchase a truck.

"You don't think you're going to be out riding around in it, do you?" Sam asked.

"No. I just need a way to get around if I have to go out. Come on, Sam, I'm going nuts here. It's been four weeks and I could do something in the office for you."

"I'll be out on my lunch break." Sam hung up.

Brody knew Sam wasn't happy about it, but he'd take Brody wherever he needed to go. There wasn't anyone else he could ask. Mark would be sleeping and there was no way he'd ask Madilyn. After the way he talked to her the last time she was here, he'd be lucky if she ever spoke to him again. He ran his hand down his face. *What the fuck is wrong with you?* She'd been there to help him and he threw it back in her face. *God! You're an idiot, Morgan.*

Later in the afternoon, Sam arrived and they headed for the car dealership. Brody picked out a black Silverado 4x4. As he drove it home, he grinned. He'd talked Sam into letting him come into the office a few days a week. Brody had to get out of the house or he'd go stir-crazy. He could get around all right, only a twinge of pain, and he no longer needed the pain meds. What he needed to do was apologize to Madilyn.

Brody pulled into the parking lot of the florist

shop. Taking a deep breath, he slowly made his way to the shop. The bell over the door rang as he entered. Sam's sister, Katie, sat at the counter. Her smile faltered a little when she saw him.

"Hello, Brody." She stood as he walked toward the counter.

"Hi Katie." He glanced around. "Is Madilyn around?"

"She didn't come in today. She said she wasn't feeling well."

Brody nodded. "All right. Thanks." He turned to go when Katie's voice stopped him.

"Don't hurt her again, Brody. Please."

Brody turned toward her. "I didn't hurt her intentionally the first time, Katie. You should know that."

Kaitlyn moved back around the counter and stared at him. "I know you didn't mean to, but you did. She was a wreck when you left. I will not see her go through it again." She placed her hands on her slim hips and glared up at him.

Brody glanced away and then back to her. "I know you mean well, Katie, and trust me, I don't want to hurt her again. I just need to see her now to apologize..."

"Yeah, I know you do." Kaitlyn took a seat on the stool behind the counter. "You were a prick, Brody. She was there to help you. Yes, she told me all about it."

"*Jesus.* I know you mean well but this is between Madilyn and me. No one else." He glared at Kaitlyn, letting her know whom he meant.

She waved her hand. "Fine. Go apologize, but

don't expect a warm welcome." Kaitlyn opened an order book and Brody knew he'd been dismissed. He strode out of the shop, got into his truck, and drove to Madilyn's apartment. Brody sat in the parking lot staring toward her place. *Get the hell out of the truck!* He sighed and got out and walked toward her apartment. Standing in front of her door, he couldn't knock. He stared at the door. *Grow some balls, Morgan!* He knocked quickly before he lost his nerve. *What are you so afraid of?* Her anger. He hated seeing her anger, especially aimed at him. Her redhead temper was deadly. He smiled, she had a lot of fire in her, and he loved that about her. The smile left his face when the door opened.

"What are you doing here, Brody?"

"Can I come in?" he asked. She looked terrible.

She sighed and opened the door to him. He strolled past her and stood in the center of the hallway. She moved past him and took a seat on her sofa. A blanket lay on it with a pillow. Tissues lay on the coffee table.

"I really don't feel well, and I look like shit." She sniffed.

"Yeah, you do." He grinned at her and took a seat when she laughed. Brody cleared his throat. "I came to apologize for the way I treated you."

"When? Four weeks ago or five years ago?"

Ouch! Brody ran his hand over his mouth. "Both."

They stared at each other until Madilyn finally nodded her head. "Apology accepted."

Brody let out a relieved sigh. "Thanks."

"Doesn't mean I've forgotten though. You hurt me. Both times, Brody. I know you're sorry about it, but you still hurt me and it's hard to forget." She shook her head. "And I was at your house to help you, and you treated me like shit. I've never been one to believe in that forgive and forget crap."

"Christ, Maddie. I'm sorry. I don't know why I acted the way I did," he groaned. "Yes, I do. I still want you and having you close to me was killing me. I know you won't let me near you again."

"I *can't* let you near me again. You tore my heart out and stomped on it. I won't go through it again."

"I get it. I won't bother you again." He stood and gazed down at her. "Even sick, you're still the most beautiful woman I know." He strode out.

* * * *

Madilyn stared at the door. She couldn't believe he left. What was he supposed to do? *You told him you wanted nothing to do with him.* She moaned. He looked so good and he would always be the love of her life. It did her no good to see anyone else. Look what happened with Zach. The jerk. Thank heaven he hadn't been around anymore. Madilyn didn't want to see him again. She made her way to the kitchen to make some hot tea. It always seemed to help with a cold. She sneezed and grabbed her head. The headache was still hanging on and her stuffed up head was making it difficult to breathe. She hated getting colds, but getting one in the summer seemed worse.

As she walked back to the living room, she glanced out the window and saw Brody standing by a black truck. She hadn't even thought of how he'd gotten there with his bike demolished. He stood leaning back against the door with his cell phone to his ear. Was he talking to a woman? She blew out a breath. What did it matter? Madilyn watched as he ran his hand over his ribs. She hadn't even asked how he was doing. The minute the man was anywhere around her, she lost all coherent thought. He glanced up and she jumped back, which was crazy since there was no way he could see her. She watched as he got into his truck. Slowly. Had he come into town just to apologize to her? Knowing Brody as well as she did, she knew he had. She heard his truck start and she gazed back out at him, smiling as she watched him put his glasses on. He wouldn't be Brody without them.

* * * *

Brody drove over to the station and entered the lobby. Betty Lou looked up with a smile, which turned into a frown when she saw Brody standing there.

"Brody Morgan, what are you doing out and about? You should be home in bed," she scolded.

"I'm fine, Betty Lou. Is Sam in his office?" Brody glanced toward the hall.

"No. He's at the Baker ranch. Someone called and reported Joe Baker was out there shooting his gun."

"Baker? Isn't he the guy who ran me off the road?" Brody asked incredulously.

"The one and only. Him and his wife, Mary,

who is as sweet as can be, moved here about five years ago. He beats her and she won't leave him." Betty Lou shook her head. "You wouldn't catch no man beating on me, I can tell you that."

Brody glanced away to hide the smile threatening. What man in his right mind would take on Betty Lou? "Is Sam out there by himself?" Brody had a bad feeling.

"Yes, and I told him to call the local police but he wouldn't hear of it."

"Give me the address. I'll go out there."

Betty Lou beamed at him. "Thank you, Brody. You're a good boy."

It had been years since Brody had been a boy but he didn't correct her. She handed him the address and after giving her a nod, he headed out. When he pulled into the driveway, he saw Sam leaning against the front of his cruiser with his arms folded. Brody parked, retrieved his weapon from the glove box, and slowly walked toward him.

"Sam? What's going on?" Brody asked.

Sam blew out a breath. "Just this idiot being his usual self."

Brody stood beside Sam. Although Sam looked relaxed, Brody knew him well enough to know he was on the edge and Brody needed to be ready. The man Sam was staring at was holding a pistol, which he had pointed at the ground.

"I'm tired of standing out here in the heat, Joe. Put the gun down. Now."

"I can shoot my own gun if I want to, Garrett," Joe Baker shouted.

"That's *Sheriff* Garrett to you and no you can't. You could hurt or even kill someone."

Joe's eyes narrowed. "There ain't no one here!"

"If you don't put the gun down, I'll shoot you and, to be honest, I'd love to do just that."

Joe's eyes widened. "You can't threaten me."

"It's not a threat. Brody? You got him?" Sam asked.

Brody aimed his weapon at Joe Baker. "I do." When Joe started to raise the gun, Brody broadened his stance. "Don't even think about it."

In the time it took Joe to glance at Brody, Sam was on him, throwing him to the ground, and handcuffing him. The entire time Joe shouted obscenities at him. Sam picked him up and pulled him to the cruiser. Mary came running over.

"I'll be down to pick you up first thing in the morning, Joe."

"He won't see the judge before ten, Mary. You'd better wait until after noon," Sam informed her and grinned at Brody.

Brody knew Sam was telling Mary to leave Joe stew in the cell awhile. After only dealing with the man for a few minutes, he knew Joe Baker deserved it.

"I'll be in tomorrow to work a few hours, Sam," Brody told him.

"Fine. I'll see you then." Sam got into his cruiser and pulled out with Brody behind him.

Since Brody needed a few things, he headed back to town. As he drove down Main Street, he decided to stop in and check on Madilyn again.

He pulled into the lot, headed for her door, and knocked. Not hearing anything, he knocked again. She was probably sleeping so he turned to go when her door opened.

"You again?"

Brody ran his hand over his mouth to cover a grin. "I wanted to see how you were feeling."

"Well, considering you were here not too long ago, I feel the same." She opened the door to allow him to enter.

"You always were a smart ass," Brody muttered as he entered the apartment.

Madilyn snorted. "I had to be around you. I couldn't let you get the better of me."

Brody grinned at her. "You look a little better than earlier. Did you drink tea?"

Madilyn laughed. "Yes. My cure all."

He shook his head as he moved toward the chair in the living room. "You actually believe tea will make you feel better."

"I'm not having this conversation with you. I won't let you put my tea down," she teased.

"Fine. Could I have some water?" Brody asked as he sat down.

Madilyn sighed. "You plan on staying a while?"

"Come on, Maddie. I just came from a bad situation." He knew the minute the words left his lips he'd said the wrong thing. She turned white. He swore softly. "I'm sorry. I shouldn't have said anything."

"No. It's fine." She flopped down on the sofa.

Brody stood. "I'll get the water. Do you need anything?" He gazed at her.

Brody

Madilyn stared up at him. "You."

"What?" Brody frowned. He couldn't have heard what he thought he heard.

She cleared her throat. "I need you. I can't deny it anymore. Just now when you told me you'd come from a bad situation, I knew I was lying to myself."

Brody squatted down in front of her. "About what?" he whispered.

"Telling myself I don't love you." Her eyes met his. She reached out and removed his glasses. "Tell me about the bad situation."

"Joe Baker was shooting a gun on his property. Sam was already there. I went out there for backup. He shouldn't have been alone out there." Brody shook his head. "Baker's the same man who ran me off the road."

Madilyn nodded. "He's a drunk, and a mean one at that."

"Maddie..."

She placed her hand over his lips. "Brody, I need to know what happened out there. How much danger were you in?"

Brody sighed. "Not much. The man was shooting up into the air but those bullets can go anywhere. Sam had it under control. I kept an eye on Baker while Sam cuffed him. That's it."

Madilyn softly laughed. "That's it? Joe Baker could've shot either one of you. He's crazy and everyone knows it."

"I know. We couldn't get him on running me off the road since his wife said he was home at the time. We all know better but with her giving him an alibi, we can't arrest him for it." He stared up at her. "Damn, you're so beautiful, Maddie."

She smiled at him. "You're the only one who gets away with calling me that."

"I always called you Maddie when we made love." Brody leaned forward and pressed his lips to hers. When she moaned, he deepened the kiss and slid his tongue between her lips. Her arms moved around his neck, her fingers splayed up through his thick hair. He moved to the sofa beside her and pulled her across his lap. Madilyn pulled her lips from his.

"You're going to get my cold," she said against his lips.

"I'll take anything I can get from you." He kissed her, his tongue moving against her lips. "Open for me, Maddie." He groaned a sound full of longing when she did. Brody slid his tongue deep into her mouth, tasting her. Laying her down on the sofa, he laid over her, cradled between her thighs, and arched, pressing his hard shaft against her. Brody moved his lips across her cheek to her neck. He'd just started nibbling when she sneezed. He froze and started laughing. Madilyn laughed with him. He raised his head and gazed down at her.

"I don't think this is going to happen. I can't have you sneezing while I'm trying to make love with you." He grinned.

Madilyn laughed. "I'm sorry." She sneezed again and started giggling.

"Yeah, every man wants this to happen," Brody muttered.

Madilyn laughed at him. "I'm sorry. How about a rain check?"

Brody's eyes met hers. "As long as you're serious about this?"

"I am. I'm not denying myself this…you, anymore."

Brody nodded. "Call me when you feel better. This could be the cold medicine talking." He stood, handed her his card, and helped her sit up. Brody picked up his glasses she'd dropped on the floor and headed toward the door. "Between you being sick and my ribs still sore, its best we put this off. I'm not sure you won't change your mind once you're thinking more clearly."

"Are you telling me I don't know what I'm saying?" Madilyn stood and put her hands on her hips and narrowed her eyes at him.

"I want you to be sure, Maddie. Just a few days ago, you hated me, and now you want me. I know for sure I want you, but I want you to be sure, too." He turned toward the door then turned back toward her. "I've never stopped loving you." He closed the door softly behind him.

Three days later, Madilyn was still sure. She sat at the desk in the back office and stared at her phone, trying to get the nerve up to call him. Picking it up, she dialed the number on his card. It rang and rang until it went to voicemail. She didn't leave a message. Where could he be? Before she lost her nerve, she called the Sheriff's department.

"Clifton County Sheriff's Department," Betty Lou answered.

"Is Sam in?" Madilyn asked.

"No, he's not. Can I take a message or would

you like to speak with one of the deputies?"

Deputies? As in plural? Madilyn knew there was only one deputy on day shift with Sam.

"What deputies?" She mentally groaned. What a stupid question.

"Deputy Stark or Deputy Morgan. Both are here."

Madilyn gave a fist pump. *Yes!* "Deputy Morgan, please." She waited while Betty Lou transferred her and hoped the older woman didn't recognize her voice. Maybe she should just hang up.

"This is Deputy Morgan, can I help you?" She froze at the sound of his voice coming over the line. "Hello?"

Madilyn cleared her throat. "Brody…"

"Maddie? Is that you? Is something wrong?"

"No. Nothing's wrong. I just wanted to tell you…" She mentally groaned. Why was this so hard?

"Tell me what?"

"I'm still sure," she whispered. The silence was deafening on the other end. Then Brody cleared his throat.

"I get off duty at five."

"I'll fix dinner. I'll pick up some steaks on the way home. I get off today at four."

"That would be nice…oh wait. Did you learn to cook?"

Madilyn burst out laughing. "I did. I'll see you later."

She glanced up when Kaitlyn entered the room. They smiled at each other. "Is everything all right, Madilyn?"

"Yes. I was just making dinner plans."

Kaitlyn got a look of pure horror on her face. "With Zach?"

Madilyn chuckled. "No. With Brody."

Kaitlyn frowned. "Are you sure that's a good idea?"

Madilyn stood. "Yes. I love him, Katie. Even if he decides to leave here again, this time I'll go with him."

"I don't want to see you hurt again, Madilyn."

"I know, Katie. I don't know what he's going to do for sure but I won't let him leave without me. It was my fault the last time for not going when he asked me to. I won't let it happen again."

Kaitlyn stared at her a few minutes then nodded. "All right, but if he hurts you I'll have Sam kick his ass."

Madilyn laughed. "That sounds good. Brody always said Sam could do it."

Chapter Five

At five o'clock Brody left the office, got into his truck and drove to Madilyn's apartment and knocked. The door opened almost immediately. They stared at each other.

"You look gorgeous, Maddie," his voice was husky as his gaze roamed over her. Her long red hair was flowing around her shoulders. She wore a light green blouse tucked into skinny jeans. On her feet were flip-flops, her toenails painted red. To him, she'd never looked more beautiful. He reached out and took a few strands of her hair between his fingers. It still felt like silk.

"Come in. I'll start the steaks..." She turned from him. Brody reached out, clasped her arm in his hand, and pulled her back against him. With her back against his chest, Brody moved her hair away before pressing his lips against her neck. Her head fell back against his shoulder. "Brody," she moaned.

Brody spun her around and took her lips in a deep kiss. He moved his tongue deep into her mouth. Her arms circled his neck as he lifted her off her feet.

"The steaks..."

"The hell with the steaks. Where's the bedroom?"

Madilyn pointed to the hallway. He scooped her up, carried her to the bedroom, put her on the bed, and then lay down beside her. Her fingers were having trouble with the buttons of his khaki shirt but she was finally able to push it from his shoulders. Her fingers ran over his hard, solid chest and down to the snap of his jeans. She could feel his hard shaft straining against the fly as she unzipped it and slid her hand inside to wrap around him. He wrapped his hand around hers.

"It'll be over before we get started if you don't stop." He put his forehead to hers.

Madilyn smiled up at him and ran her hands up his rippled stomach to his hard pecs. Her fingertip traced the tattoo of her name.

"I thought you'd have this removed by now."

"Never," he whispered before kissing her again.

Madilyn's fingers plowed through his hair and pulled him to her as she rose up to kiss him. "I've missed you so much. I was so stupid. I should have..."

Brody interrupted her with a kiss. "It's in the past. We're here now, and I need you so much." His hand traveled to the buttons of her blouse. He took it off her and tossed it to the floor. His mouth slid across her cheek to her ear, where he moved his tongue around the shell of her ear, then moved to her neck all the while unhooking her bra. Madilyn gasped.

"I see you haven't lost your touch," she whispered.

Brody chuckled. "You always wore these with the front hook." He stared into her eyes. "You did that for me, didn't you?"

"Yes," she breathed against his lips.

Brody pulled her up and removed the bra. It

also hit the floor. He stared at her breasts. He swallowed hard and closed his eyes before gazing into hers again. "You're still perfect. So very perfect," he whispered as he lowered his head to take her nipple into his mouth. His tongue swirled around it making it harden into a tight peak. He gently pulled at it with his teeth and then sucked it into his mouth.

Madilyn's head tilted back as she moaned. Her hand snaked inside his jeans again and wrapped around him. "Brody...please."

Brody moved away from her and stripped. Madilyn twisted out of her jeans and lay before him in black panties. He groaned as he stared down at her. "You're still the most beautiful woman I know," he said again as he pulled her panties off.

* * * *

She held her arms out to him and he went into them willingly. He pressed his lips to hers, kissing her deeply. His hard cock was straining against his boxer briefs. His lips left hers and traveled down her neck to her breast. Cupping one in his hand, he moved his thumb over her nipple as he took the other one into his mouth and sucked. His hand moved down her body to her red curls and he moved his fingers down her wet folds then inserted two while his thumb rubbed against her clitoris. Brody moved down her body, kissing her stomach, running his tongue around her belly button before moving lower, and dipping it beneath her red curls at the juncture of her thighs. He used his thumbs to pull her open to him and lifted her legs over his shoulders. His tongue lapped at her clitoris. As he continued his assault, he felt her tightening around his fingers right before she cried out his name.

"My name's tattooed on your hip," he said in awe.

"Yes. I had it done right before you left."

"I wish—"

"Let it go," Madilyn whispered.

Brody moved up her body and kissed her. Then he groaned and laid his forehead against hers. "Shit. I don't have a condom."

"Nightstand." Madilyn pointed to the small bedside table.

Brody froze. "You have condoms?"

She grinned up at him. "I picked them up today."

His breath rushed out in a laugh. "Thank you." He kissed her quickly and reached into the table to retrieve one. Madilyn took it from him and rolled it down over him. "You're killing me, baby."

Madilyn laughed softly as she wrapped her legs around his waist. "Quit stalling, Morgan."

Brody grit his teeth as he moved into her. She was so tight. "Maddie, I don't want to hurt you," he groaned when she lifted her hips to take him in deeper.

"You won't, Brody," she said before nipping his neck.

Brody pushed into her. She cried out but then wrapped her arms tight around his neck. When he started moving, she kept in rhythm with him. His hand slipped under her butt to pull her tighter against him. His lips pressed to hers, his tongue dipped into the honeyed depth of her mouth. When Madilyn took his bottom lip between her teeth, he almost lost it. Her hands roamed down his back to his butt, where she dug her nails into him. He moved harder and faster against her. Her breathing became deeper and her cheeks flushed. Brody felt her tighten around him just as she cried out his name again. Brody followed her over, groaning her name against her neck. He raised his head and kissed her then rolled to his back beside her. He glanced over to her.

"You okay?" he asked.

"Yep," she told him. "You?"

Brody burst out laughing. "I'm fantastic."

Madilyn laughed and rolled over to face him. She placed her hands on his chest, rested her chin on them, and gazed into his eyes. "It was always good with us, wasn't it?"

Brody smiled at her. "Always." Then he frowned. "Was it good with Johnson?"

Madilyn sat up. "I can't believe you just asked me that!" She scrambled off the bed and put her clothes on and scooped his clothes off the floor, and threw them at him. "Get out."

"Maddie..." Brody started as he got off the bed.

She strode over to him and pointed her finger at him. "*Don't.*" She said through clenched teeth then spun on her heel and strode out the door.

Brody hopped around trying to pull his jeans on. *What the fuck is wrong with you?* He asked himself. When he finally got dressed, he headed for the kitchen, only to see her putting the steaks into the fridge. He walked up behind her and put his hands on her shoulders. She jerked away and spun around.

"You're still here?" She raised an eyebrow at him.

"Maddie, I'm sorry. I didn't mean—"

"Didn't mean what, Brody? To say it out loud? To butt into my personal life? What? What didn't you mean?" her voice rose.

Brody sighed and ran his fingers through his hair. "All of the above."

"That's what I thought." She pointed to the door. "Go."

He stared at her, but he knew she'd made up her mind, he huffed and walked out, slamming the door behind him.

* * * *

Madilyn stared at the door he'd just gone out of. How could he ask her something like that after what they'd shared? She picked up a pillow and threw it at the door. *Damn you, Brody Morgan!* She was so angry she could hardly see. Madilyn stalked toward the kitchen and halted. Why would he do that? She didn't ask him about past lovers. Not that she'd slept with Zach, that wasn't the point. The point was, Brody had no right, whatsoever, to ask her such a question. She clenched her fists.

"Arrgghhh!" she growled. The man was going to drive her insane. Madilyn paused. He was jealous. Pure and simple. Brody was jealous over her seeing Zach. She didn't care how jealous he was, asking her such a question was simply wrong. She'd never ask him about past lovers

and she was positive he'd slept with his share over the past five years.

A knock sounded at her door. She ran to it and pulled it open, thinking she'd see Brody standing there. A man she'd never seen before stood before her. She quickly stepped behind the door, using it as a shield.

"Can I help you?" Madilyn asked him. He was a very attractive man.

The man smiled. "Is Caroline here?"

Madilyn gave a relieved sigh. "You have the wrong apartment."

He frowned. "This isn't apartment B on the sixth floor?"

Madilyn laughed. "This is B on the fifth floor."

The man chuckled. "One flight up. I'm so sorry to have bothered you." He nodded. "Have a nice day, ma'am."

Madilyn smiled and shook her head as she closed the door. She walked to the living room and halted. Apartment B on the sixth floor was Max and Sherry Colter. No one named Caroline lived there. Madilyn shrugged. Perhaps he was meeting a woman named Caroline there. She nodded. That had to be it. Although she hadn't eaten, she wasn't hungry. Brody had killed her appetite. Sighing, she headed for the shower. It looked like it was going to be an early night.

* * * *

Brody swore the entire ride home. How could he have been so stupid? Why had Johnson even popped into his head? Maddie was right. It was none of his business. They'd been apart for a long time and although he hated the thought of her being with another man, he couldn't blame her if she had. He sure as hell hadn't been a saint for the years he'd been gone.

God damn it! He pulled into the driveway of his home, spinning the tires and throwing gravel everywhere. Throwing it in park, he hopped out and strode into the house, slamming the door behind him. Brody took his glasses off, tossed them on the kitchen counter, and pinched the bridge of his nose. Striding to the bedroom, he undressed and then headed into the bathroom to take a shower. He should still be in bed with Madilyn. It had been so good, just as always. He was getting hard thinking about her again. *Damn it!* He punched the wall and then swore again, when he hurt his hand. After his shower, Brody wrapped a towel around his waist, and entered the bedroom. After pulling on a pair of sweat pants, he walked to the living room, sat on the sofa, and watched television. It was going to be a long night.

* * * *

Wilson Delgado sat in the car keeping an eye on the apartment Madilyn Young lived in. U S Marshal Brody Morgan apparently wasn't coming back tonight. Lover's quarrel? He snorted. It really didn't matter. He was going to take Madilyn Young away from Morgan just as Morgan had taken Abby away from him. His fist hit the steering wheel. Brody Morgan was going to pay for making him kill his wife. *His* wife who Morgan slept with. Delgado killed his wife because she'd screwed around with Morgan and Morgan arrested him, but it was never proven

Delgado killed her so he was let go. He'd hired the best private detective money could buy to find out all he could about Morgan's past and where he could've gone. Now, here he sat in a rinky-dink town biding his time. He had no desire to kill Morgan. No, that would be entirely too easy. He'd take away the one thing Morgan loved more than his own life. Madilyn Young.

* * * *

Monday morning came entirely too early for Madilyn. She had to open the shop. Kaitlyn would be in later. Madilyn tossed and turned any time she tried to sleep over the weekend. Damn Brody Morgan. He hadn't even called. What was that all about? He should've called to apologize again. Sighing, Madilyn left her apartment and walked to the shop. It was going to be another scorcher and working in the greenhouse was going to be murder. She unlocked the shop and turned the lights on. It wouldn't open for another hour but she wanted to get started on the day. There were quite a few tourists in town. Madilyn knew they'd eventually head for the greenhouse since they seemed to go into every store in town. The proprietors didn't seem to mind though. It brought in business.

An hour later, she headed toward the door to unlock it, and saw Brody standing on the other side. She stopped in her tracks and glared at him through the glass. He glanced away from her and she was sure it was to hide a grin. Madilyn unlocked the door but blocked the doorway.

"We're not open yet."

"I believe the hours on the door show you open at ten." He glanced at the watch on his wrist. "And according to my watch. It's a minute after."

Sighing, she held the door open for him. He strode in past her. She closed her eyes. He smelled fantastic. "What do you want Brody? I have a lot to do."

"I want to buy some flowers."

Her heart hit her stomach. He was buying flowers for another woman already. She spun on her heel, moved behind the counter, and picked up her pen. "What kind?"

"The kind that say I was an ass and I'm sorry," he said quietly.

Her head snapped up. "You're going to need a lot of flowers for that."

"Money is no object. She's worth it."

Madilyn moved around the counter and stood in front of him. "Is she?"

Brody reached out and took a few strands of her hair between his fingers. "Yes, she is."

"You had no right asking me such a question."

He huffed. "I know. It just came out." He shrugged. "Thinking of you with him made me jealous."

"I've never slept with Zach."

"What?" Brody narrowed his eyes at her.

"You just assumed it. You know what they say about assuming." Madilyn bit her lip to keep from smiling.

"You dated him for almost a year."

"And not once did he make me feel the way you do." She ran her hands up his arms and around his neck. "No one ever has. In all the time you've been gone, I haven't been with anyone else."

Brody's eyebrows rose. "No one?"

Madilyn shook her head. "No one. Can you say the same?"

"No, but they didn't mean anything to me. It was just sex. I've never loved anyone but you." He lowered his head and pressed his lips to hers. They sprang apart when the bell over the door announced a visitor. They both looked over to see Kaitlyn. Madilyn knew by the look on her face that something was wrong. Brody must have seen it too since he kissed her forehead then smiled at Kaitlyn and left.

Kaitlyn moved behind the counter and picked up the order book. Madilyn could tell she'd been crying.

"Katie? I thought you weren't coming in until later?"

Kaitlyn didn't raise her eyes. "I wanted to get started on the orders," her voice cracked.

Madilyn moved toward her and touched her arm. "What happened? What did he do now?"

Kaitlyn raised her gaze to her. "He didn't come home last night. I know he was with…her."

"Katie, you need to divorce him. He treats you like dirt." Madilyn hated seeing her friend hurt. Everyone in Clifton knew her husband had a mistress he spent more time with than his wife.

"He won't divorce me and even if he did, I can't support myself."

"You have Sam. He'd take care of you."

Kaitlyn shook her head. "I won't ask Sam or my parents for help."

Madilyn knew it was the end of the conversation. Kaitlyn wouldn't leave her husband because she believed in her wedding vows although Kevin didn't. He'd had a mistress before he married Kaitlyn and although a good many people tried to tell her, she refused to believe it, but she believed it now.

Madilyn went to work in the greenhouse while Kaitlyn worked on flower arrangements. Madilyn was sad her friend was hurting. They worked in virtual silence through the day, only speaking when customers came in.

Although Madilyn had lived through a lot of heartache, she couldn't imagine what Kaitlyn was feeling. Madilyn's mother died when she was five years old, so she never knew her. Her father had been her entire world until he'd brought home a rookie officer for dinner one night. Brody Morgan stole her breath away. She fell in love and he'd felt the same but when her father was shot and killed by a man he'd pulled over one night, she lived in constant fear Brody would also be killed in the line of duty. Madilyn begged him to leave the force but Brody refused, saying the probability of it happening to him in the town of Clifton was slim to none. He'd convinced her and they were happy until the night he told her he was going to join the Marshals in Butte and wanted her to go with him. She couldn't do it and five years were wasted. Now her friend's heart was breaking and there wasn't anything Madilyn could do to help her. Seeing Kaitlyn in the emotional pain she was in tore her apart. If there was something she could do to ease the pain, she'd do it in a heartbeat. Kevin Parker was scum and Kaitlyn deserved so much better.

* * * *

Brody sat at his desk filling out a report on a car accident. His mind was not on his work. It was on Madilyn. God, he loved her. She'd always been in the back of his mind in the years he was gone. Getting involved with other women did nothing to make her fade away. He put the pen down, took his glasses off, and rubbed his eyes. There was one woman in particular he never should have been involved with. If she'd been honest from the beginning things would have turned out differently. What a mess that turned out to be. His office phone rang.

"Deputy Morgan."

"Come to my office," Sam said in a clipped voice and hung up.

Damn it! Brody knew time had just run out. Sam wanted the details of his leaving the Marshals. Brody stood and headed for Sam's office. Brody knocked on the doorjamb of Sam's office. When Sam glanced up and waved him in, he knew it couldn't be good.

"Come in and close the door," Sam told him.

No. It wasn't going to be good. Brody took a seat across from Sam and waited. It didn't take long.

"It's time you told me why you left the Marshals." Sam sat back and folded his arms.

Shit! Brody hated telling Sam about this, but he also knew Sam could make a phone call and talk to Michael Holt, Brody's superior, and find out. He'd rather be the one to tell him. Taking a deep breath, he began to tell Sam what happened.

"I was involved with a woman for six months before I found out she was married." He stopped when Sam swore. "I should've known, but she hid it well."

"Were you in love with her?" Sam asked.

"No. There's only one woman I'll ever love and that's Madilyn. Thing is, I never thought I'd see Maddie again and I wanted to get on with my life. I wanted to get married and have kids." He shrugged. "If I couldn't have it with Maddie, I needed to find someone I could have it with. I met Abby Bishop at a bar and we immediately hit it off. She didn't tell me she was married or I wouldn't have messed with her." He shifted in his chair. "One night her husband, Wilson Delgado, came to see me and told me to stay the hell away from her. I told him I never knew she was married. Of course, he didn't believe me and told me if I didn't stay away I'd regret it. I told him I was a U.S. Marshal. Hell, he laughed and said it didn't matter. Needless to say, I called her and broke it off." Brody ran his hand down his face. Sam didn't say anything, just stared at him until he continued. "She took it bad and swore she'd leave her husband. I didn't want to hear any of it. I knew she was lying. Christ, all she did was lie to me." Brody swallowed hard and glanced away. "I have better instincts, Sam. I don't know how I missed it. She never wanted to meet anywhere but at my apartment and we went to dinner out of town and she used her maiden name." He glanced back to Sam. "I should have seen it."

"Go on," Sam told him.

Brody took a deep breath. "A month later she was dead."

Sam leaned forward. "Why the hell didn't you tell me all of this when you called me?"

"I wanted to get past it. I accused her husband. I still think he killed her but we couldn't find any evidence. None, Sam. They found her body in Wyoming. Animals had gotten to her..." Brody cleared his throat. "I couldn't let him get away with it. I followed him. Everywhere the son of a bitch would go, I followed. He reported me to Holt. You know how Holt is. He exploded."

"I'm sure he did." Sam shook his head. "You're not telling me everything. Holt had to tell you to back off before he went off. How long did you keep following Delgado after you were told not to?"

"Another week. I know, Sam." Brody said before Sam could interrupt. "I kept telling Holt, Delgado was guilty and of course without evidence I had no proof." Brody shook his head. "Holt told me I either stop harassing Delgado or I leave the Marshals." He gave a humorless laugh. "You see how that turned out. I couldn't let it go."

"Why are you so sure Delgado killed her?"

"Abby didn't have any enemies and Delgado knew she was having an affair. I know he did it. I know it with every fiber of my being. He's like a crime boss but no one can get him on anything."

"I trust your intuition on this, but you should

have been thinking with the head on your shoulders instead of the one between your legs when you met her." Sam sighed. "All right. I'm going to let it go. But I better not hear of you going back to Butte to confront Delgado or you'll be out of another job. Is that understood?"

"Yes. I'm done with it. He'll rot in hell, that's good enough for me."

"It sure as hell better be, Brody."

Brody stood and stuck his hand out. "You have my word, Sam."

After a slight hesitation, Sam shook his hand. Brody left the office and headed home. Talking about it with Sam brought up all the bad memories. He couldn't get it out of his head again. Abby hadn't deserved to die. Brody knew Delgado killed her but he couldn't prove it. She'd been shot execution style, in the back of the head. Delgado may not have pulled the trigger but Brody knew he'd ordered the hit. The man was a pig and deserved to go to prison for killing her. He shook his head. He had to let it go. He lost a job he loved because of his obsession over it. The thing was he needed to tell Madilyn about it. He wanted no secrets between them. He pulled off the road and turned around to head for her apartment.

Brody knocked and waited. She didn't answer and his heart hit his stomach. He pounded harder. A door behind him opened.

"She ain't home. Quit pounding on the damn door," an old man yelled from across the hall.

Brody sighed. "I didn't mean to disturb you. I...need to talk to her."

"Can't talk to her if she ain't home. It's Monday. She works late on Mondays." The old man slammed the door.

"Yeah, thanks," Brody muttered. He walked to his truck and drove to the flower shop. When he walked in, customers were everywhere. Kaitlyn waved her hand toward the greenhouse so he strolled out there to find Madilyn. She was talking with a customer. When she saw him, she smiled but continued to talk with the customer. Brody leaned against the doorjamb and watched her. He could feel the sweat rolling down between his shoulder blades. How the hell did she do this? It was hotter than hell out in the greenhouse but Madilyn looked as if the heat didn't bother her at all. Finally, the customer left, and she moved toward him, smiling.

"What are you doing here?"

Brody straightened up and cleared his throat. "Can we talk tonight?'

Madilyn frowned. "Yes. Is everything all right?"

"I want to tell you why I left the Marshals."

"All right. I'd like to hear it. I don't get home until around six tonight."

"That's fine. I'll bring a pizza. You still like mushrooms on yours?"

"Yes and if you still like green peppers, do half of each." She smiled at him.

Brody nodded. "All right. I'll see you tonight." He turned to move away.

"Brody."

He turned to face her. "Yes?"

"It'll be fine." Madilyn tried to reassure him.

Brody nodded. "I hope so, Maddie. I sure as hell hope so." He smiled and walked off.

* * * *

Madilyn frowned as she watched him sauntering away from her. She didn't have a good feeling about what he was going to say and she hoped it didn't change anything between them. She shook her head. Nothing could change her feelings for Brody. If the fact of him leaving her five years ago hadn't changed anything then nothing else could. She nibbled on her bottom lip. At least she hoped not. He seemed a little uneasy about whatever he had to tell her. The butterflies in her stomach were telling her it wasn't going to be something she wanted to hear. Maybe it would be better if he didn't tell her anything at all. She'd never seen him nervous before, not even the night he told her he was joining the Marshals. He'd been confident, but now he seemed hesitant. As if he knew it was something she wouldn't forgive him for. What could he possibly have done to make him think that way? He had to know she'd love him no matter what. Yes, she'd love him, but would she stay with him?

Was it something so terrible, he was afraid she'd never forgive him? Madilyn was afraid to hear what he had to say. Should she call him and tell him she didn't want to hear what it was about? It didn't matter to her what his reasons for leaving the Marshals was, she didn't need to know. It was between him and the Marshals. She didn't need to know. Making up her mind, she picked up her cell phone but a customer came in and the rest of the day passed quickly. She never got the chance to call him. He was going to tell her and knowing Brody as she did, she knew if he wanted her to know, he'd tell her no matter how she felt about it. With something that important, he'd tie her down to make her listen if he had to. She shrugged, knowing she'd listen but it wouldn't change how she felt about him.

Chapter Six

As Brody drove to Madilyn's later in the evening, his stomach was in knots. He wasn't sure how she was going to take the fact he'd been involved with a married woman. It didn't matter whether he knew or not, she'd frown upon it. She said cheating was something she could never forgive. *Shit!* He ran his hand down his face. How was he going to tell her? Would she even believe him when he told her he hadn't known Abby was married? Brody shook his head. Maybe he should have kept it to himself. What she didn't know wouldn't hurt her. He never believed in that saying, because eventually the person found out and when that happened, all hell broke loose. He'd never lied to Madilyn before and he wasn't about to start now. Brody knew he'd feel better after telling her just as he did after telling Sam.

He pulled into the parking lot and strolled to her apartment. God, he hoped this went well. Taking a deep breath, he blew it out as he knocked on the door. She pulled it open and smiled at him and his heart hit his stomach. He loved her so much and after losing her five years ago, he swore he never would again.

"Hi. Come in." She opened the door for him to enter.

"Hi." He quickly kissed her lips and strolled to the living room. She entered behind him and took a seat on the sofa. He paced.

"Is it so bad? What you have to tell me?" she whispered.

Brody ran his fingers through his hair. "It's not pretty but I want you to know about it before we go on with our lives. I don't want it to surface later and you get angry I didn't tell you."

Madilyn nodded. "All right. Sit down, Brody. You're making me nervous."

Brody sat on the sofa next to her and took her hand in his. "Before I say anything, I want you to promise you'll listen to all of it before jumping to conclusions."

She seemed to hesitate but finally nodded. "I promise. Go ahead."

"I had an affair with a married woman." When she tried to pull her hand away, he held it tighter. "You said you'd listen." She huffed and nodded. "Good. I didn't know she was married. She hid it from me for six months. I should have known. I have better instincts but I didn't see it."

"Because you were in love with her?"

"No. I was never in love with her. At first, it was just sex then I thought I'd try to make a go of it with her. I thought I'd never be with you again, and I wanted to get married and have kids." He shook his head. "Her husband, Wilson Delgado, came to see me. Told me to stay the hell away from his wife or I'd regret it. I told him I didn't know she was married. He laughed and said he didn't believe me. I also told him I was a U S Marshal and he just laughed harder. It didn't matter he said. I called Abby later that night to break it off with her. She took it hard and swore she'd leave him. Of course, I didn't believe her. I mean, all she did was lie to me. A month later, she was dead. I know her husband killed her but I couldn't prove it. He's a very powerful man in Butte. He's involved with the mob but just like anything else, it's never been proven. I was let go from the Marshals because I couldn't let it go. I followed Delgado everywhere and he eventually reported me to my supervisor. When Holt warned me the first time I didn't listen, I continued to follow Delgado. I was obsessed with proving him the killer. As I told Sam, he may not have pulled the trigger but he had something to do with it. I know it in my bones."

Madilyn stood and moved away from him. "Why were you so obsessed with proving him the killer? Why did it matter so much to you?"

Brody jumped up. "Why did it matter so much? Because a woman was murdered."

"Is that all it was, or was it because you did love her and wanted to avenge her death?"

"I wasn't in love with her, Madilyn," Brody said through clenched teeth.

She nodded. "Then why not just let someone else investigate it? Why were you so hell bent on getting him for it? And I find it hard to believe you didn't know she was married, Brody."

"Son of a bitch. I knew you would say that. It's why I battled with myself all the way here. I didn't know. She hid it from me."

"For six months?"

"Yes, for six months. Look, I beat myself up for it every day because she's dead and it's my fault. If I'd known she was married, I never would have gotten involved with her. I do not get involved with married women."

"Apparently, you do."

Brody stared at her. "I can't believe you said that. You know better."

"Do I? You've been gone for five years, Brody. How do I know what you're like now?"

"Well, if you'd have gone with me, you'd know and none of this would have happened."

Madilyn laughed without humor. "So it's my fault your lover's dead? Don't pull that shit on me. You screwed around with a married woman and she's dead. You couldn't let it go and it cost you your job. A job you left me for. If your supervisor told you to let it go then you should have, but you didn't. To me, it sounds like you cared for her way more than you're willing to admit."

"I cared about her, yes but I wasn't in love with her. You're the only woman I'll love."

"You thought about marrying her," Madilyn said softly.

"Only because I thought I'd never see you again. I didn't know if you'd gotten married and had children or what. It was five years. I was sure you'd moved on and I needed to."

Madilyn shook her head. "All you ever had to do was ask someone."

"You're serious? Did you ever once ask Sam about me?" Brody stared at her. "Did you?" he shouted.

"No. You left me. That told me I wasn't important enough to you."

"You're sprouting such bullshit and you know it. I asked you to go with me. You refused. We've wasted five years."

"You didn't. You were ready to move on," Madilyn shouted.

"I feel like I'm banging my head against a fucking wall." He strode to her and clasped her arms. "I asked you to go with me. Don't put this on me. You wouldn't go. It may not be your fault about Abby, but it is your fault we lost five years."

Madilyn jerked away from him. "Get out. I'm done. I've had enough of this. I don't believe you about not knowing she was married. I will not take the entire blame for ending it five years ago. You left. If you'd have loved me you would have stayed."

"And you should have supported my decision to become a Marshal. You didn't love me enough. If you had, you'd have taken the chance and gone with me. I'm still here. I wasn't shot or killed like you were so sure would happen. You ruined what we had. I didn't." He strode to the door and left, slamming it behind him.

* * * *

Madilyn stood at the counter helping a customer when the bell rang over the door. She glanced up and smiled when she saw her friends enter. Emma Stone was a longtime friend. The two women with her were new friends but she loved them just the same. Becca Stone and Olivia Roberts were new to Clifton. They'd been there for three years and Becca owned the Clifton Bed and Breakfast, which is what brought all the business into the small town. Becca married Jake Stone two years ago and Emma was married to Jake's brother, Gabe. Olivia wasn't married but she moved to Clifton since she and Becca were best friends. Closer than most sisters.

"Hey, girl. We brought lunch." Emma smiled as she held up a large bag.

"I knew I smelled food. Burgers from the diner?" Madilyn grinned.

"Yes and onion rings and fries. We weren't sure which you wanted. Where's Katie?" Becca glanced around.

"In the back office. I'll get her when I finish with Mrs. Holden," Madilyn told them.

"We'll be in the break room," Emma told her.

Madilyn nodded and waited while Mrs. Holden looked through flower arrangements then she joined her friends in the break room. They had the food out, waiting for her. She noticed Kaitlyn was missing.

"Where's Katie?"

"She was here for a minute then said she needed to use the bathroom," Olivia told her.

Madilyn nodded and sat down. Kaitlyn entered the room and sat back down. Madilyn knew by the look on her face that something was wrong. She reached out and touched her hand.

"Katie? What is it? You look so pale."

The women stopped what they were doing to gaze at Kaitlyn. "We're all friends here, Katie. You can tell us. You know it won't go any further than this room," Emma said softly.

"I'm pregnant," Kaitlyn whispered.

No one knew what to say. They knew about Kaitlyn's husband. How he cheated on her with his mistress. They knew, without being told, he wouldn't be happy about the pregnancy.

"I want the baby. It's not that I'm sad about it, it's just Kevin will think I did it on purpose, even though..." Katie stopped and shook her head.

"For what reason? You stay with him in spite of his cheating," Olivia said.

"Olivia Rene Roberts." Becca chastised her friend.

Olivia shrugged. "I'm sure you were all thinking the same thing. I just happen to have the balls to say it."

Kaitlyn laughed softly. "Leave it to Liv. She's right, though. He'll want me to have an abortion. He doesn't want kids. I always have." She shook her head. "Before we got married, he said he wanted children then when I brought it up on our year anniversary he told me he changed his mind. I was devastated." Her hand ran over her still flat stomach. "I want this baby and I don't care what Kevin says and the fact it wasn't conceived in love doesn't matter to me."

"Good for you," Becca said.

They dug into their food, laughing and talking when they heard the front bell ring, announcing a customer. When Kaitlyn started to rise, Madilyn told her she'd get them. She walked into the front of the shop and came to a stop when she saw Sam standing there.

"Sam? Is something wrong?" She prayed there wasn't.

"Not with Brody. I need to speak with my sister."

Madilyn knew by the look on his face it wasn't

good news. "She's in the break room." She turned to lead Sam back. She took her seat at the table while Sam hovered in the doorway.

"Katie, we need to go to your office. I need to speak with you."

Kaitlyn stood. "What is it Sam? Is it Mom or Dad?"

Sam shook his head. "Just come with me, please." He held his hand out to her. Kaitlyn put her hand in his and after giving the women a nod, Sam led her to the office.

"What's that all about?" Emma muttered.

Madilyn shook her head. "No clue."

"I know this isn't the time to say it but damn, Sam Garrett is so fucking hot." Olivia sighed. The women glared at her. She shrugged. "Just sayin'."

A few minutes later, Sam stood in the doorway. They gazed up at him. "Katie could use you girls for a while. Kevin's been killed in a car accident. Along with his mistress," the last he said through clenched teeth. "Katie took it a lot better than I thought, but it could be shock. She's in her office." He left them all staring at the door then they jumped up and ran to the back office. Kaitlyn sat at the desk, staring into space. She glanced over to them but didn't say anything. Madilyn crouched down beside her.

"Katie? Are you all right?"

"Kevin's dead."

"We know. Sam told us. Do you need us to do anything for you? One of us could take you home."

"The day after I find out I'm pregnant I lose my

husband who wouldn't have wanted the baby. How ironic is that?"

"Come on, Katie. We'll take you home." Becca helped her up.

"I'll take care of the shop, Katie, and I'll be over after work if you want me to."

"I'd love it, Madilyn. I don't want to be alone too much. I don't think it's sunk in yet."

Becca wrapped her arm around Kaitlyn's shoulders and led her away. Madilyn cried. Not for Kevin, he didn't deserve the tears, but for her friend who was hurting. She'd go stay with Kaitlyn for a few days. It's what friends did.

* * * *

Three days later, almost the entire town was at the cemetery. They weren't there for Kevin, they were there to support Kaitlyn. Sam stood on one side of her while their parents stood on the other. Madilyn stood beside Sam and let her gaze roam the crowd until she spotted Brody. He was staring at her. She couldn't tear her eyes away from him. No matter what he'd told her, she loved him, and she wanted him in her life. She'd take whatever time she could get with him. He'd been telling the truth, she knew it now. He'd never, knowingly, fool around with a married woman. It wasn't his style. There were too many single women out there. Why would he chance something like that? No, she mentally shook her head, he'd told her the truth, and the thing is, he really didn't have to tell her anything. He did because he loved her and wanted all the past behind them. She smiled sadly, as she looked across the gravesite at him. He smiled back.

When the service broke up, Sam led Kaitlyn away, and Madilyn moved toward Brody. He stood in one spot waiting for her. She stopped in front of him and gazed up at him.

"Is Katie all right?" Brody asked.

"Yes. I stayed with her the past few nights. I think she's glad it's over."

Brody nodded, and glanced away from her then back. "He was an ass."

"Everyone thought the same thing. Katie just didn't want to see it." Madilyn shook her head. "I don't know what she's going to do now though. She's pregnant."

Brody's eyebrows rose. "She was still sleeping with him? Even though he was screwing around?"

Madilyn chewed on her bottom lip and shook her head. "He raped her last month. She told me the other night when I was staying with her."

"Son of a bitch!" Brody roared. Several people turned to glare at him but he didn't care. "Does Sam know?" he whispered.

"Not yet. Katie hasn't told him she's pregnant yet."

"All I can say is it's a damn good thing the bastard's dead or Sam would kill him."

"I know. She said she'd tell him tonight. She's staying at the ranch with him for a while."

"Is she telling him about the pregnancy or rape?"

"Both." Madilyn reached for his hand. "I'm sorry about what I said, Brody. I know you were telling the truth about the married woman."

He nodded. "I was hoping you'd eventually

realize it."

"I'm sorry—"

"It's all right. I'm sure it was hard to believe but it was the truth. I've never lied to you before, I won't start now." Brody interrupted her.

"I know. I guess jealousy reared its ugly head."

Brody snorted. "Tell me about it."

They started walking across the cemetery together when Brody halted and quickly glanced around. Shaking his head, he took her elbow and continued.

"What was that for?" Madilyn whispered, as they got closer to other people.

"Nothing. Just a feeling."

Madilyn glanced at him. "What kind of feeling?"

"Never mind." Brody shook his head.

"All right."

They got into their separate cars and drove to Sam's ranch where everyone was meeting after the funeral. When they entered the back door, Kaitlyn came toward them, and took Madilyn's hand.

"Can I talk to you?"

Madilyn glanced at Brody. "Of course you can, Katie."

Kaitlyn nodded and led her through the house to a back bedroom. Once inside, they sat together on the bed. She took a deep breath and looked at Madilyn.

"I want you to be with me when I tell my parents and Sam about my pregnancy. I can't do it alone."

Madilyn stared at her in shock but Kaitlyn

was her friend. "All right. Is that all you're going to tell them?"

Kaitlyn smiled sadly. "They'll want to know why I slept with Kevin when he was screwing around on me. Sam's never understood how or why I stayed with Kevin. He was always telling me to leave him. I told him I believed in my vows but mostly it was because I had nowhere to go and I couldn't support myself. You and I both know the shop doesn't pay much. Knowing Sam, he would have made me live here with him, and there was no way I'd do it. Sam needs his privacy."

"I know, Katie. I'm here for you. When do you want to do this?"

"Once everyone leaves. I'm still staying here. I can't be alone in the house right now."

Madilyn wrapped her arms around her. She hadn't seen Kaitlyn shed one tear for Kevin. Of course, Madilyn wouldn't either if a man treated her in such a way. No one cried for Kevin. Everyone in town felt nothing but disdain for the man. He blatantly belittled his wife by his behavior. Both women jerked when the door opened, and Sam poked his head in.

"Is everything all right?"

Madilyn smiled. "Yes. Just a little alone time."

"All right. Take your time." He closed the door.

"I'm so scared to tell him. Knowing Sam, he'll dig Kevin up just to kick the shit out of him." Kaitlyn snorted then started to giggle.

Madilyn couldn't stop the laugh from erupting. "Oh, God. He so would." They laughed until tears rolled down their cheeks.

* * * *

Brody stood in the living room sipping on iced tea. He hated these things. Who didn't? He never knew what to do or say so he always stayed back from the other people. He saw Jake Stone moving toward him.

"Brody, it's been a while. Too bad we had to meet up again for a funeral." Jake stuck his hand out.

Brody grinned and shook his hand. "How are you, Jake? I couldn't believe it when Sam told me you and Gabe are both married now."

Jake chuckled. "A redhead stole my heart. What can I say?" He glanced over to his wife, and smiled.

"She's a beauty, that's for sure." Brody teased.

Jake laughed. "I know, and you teasing me doesn't bother me in the least. I know she loves me."

Gabe Stone joined them, and stuck his hand out to Brody. "How the hell are you, Morgan?"

"I'm good, Gabe. What about you? I can't believe you married Emma Conner."

"Have you seen Emma?" Gabe joked. "Our daughter is the image of her momma."

Brody shook his head. "I haven't seen Emma in five years." He gazed around the room. "That is not Emma Conner."

Gabe looked over his shoulder, and smiled. "Yep. That's my wife."

"Damn, you two are lucky men. Is Wyatt married too?"

Jake snorted. "No. He came damned close but

Stephanie Taylor broke his heart three years ago. He's sworn off marriage now."

Brody chuckled. "I'm sure that makes a lot of women happy."

The men laughed until Becca narrowed her eyes at them. Jake cleared his throat, and Gabe glanced away. Brody chuckled.

"I see who the boss is," Brody teased.

Jake grinned. "I don't deny it."

Gabe chuckled. "I don't either. All Emma has to do is give me that look all women know, and I know I'd better straighten up."

"Who's the beauty talking with Ryder?"

"Becca's best friend, Olivia Roberts. She could make a sailor blush, but we all love her," Jake said.

"Except for Wyatt. He steers clear of her," Gabe added.

"Wyatt steers clear of a beautiful woman?" Brody was shocked.

"He's skittish. Liv wants him, and doesn't care if he knows it or not. She's made her intentions clear." Jake shook his head. "She'll get him too. Of that I have no doubt."

Brody grinned. "Might be fun to watch."

The men laughed again until Becca headed toward them. She glared up at Jake. "In case you all haven't noticed, we're here for Katie. She just buried her husband. This isn't a party." She bit her lip. "Although it should be."

Brody burst out laughing and looked at Jake. "I like her."

Jake pulled Becca toward him. "Yeah, I kind of like her too. Red, this is Brody Morgan. Brody, my wife, Becca."

Brody shook her hand and grinned at her. "Nice to meet you, Becca."

"I've heard all about you, Brody Morgan. You hurt Madilyn again, and you're dead meat."

Brody raised his eyebrows and glanced at Jake and Gabe, who were both trying not to laugh. "I won't hurt her again, Becca."

Becca nodded. Olivia and Emma stepped up beside her. Olivia looked him up and down and it took every ounce of his willpower not to squirm.

"So. You're Brody, huh? I'm Olivia Roberts. Liv to my friends. I'm really someone you don't want to piss off, so be good to Madilyn." She grinned at him.

Brody ran his hand over his mouth. "Holy shit." He looked at Jake. "She's serious."

"Liv tells it like it is. I'd tread lightly if I were you." Jake grinned.

Ryder Wolfe laughed. "It's good to see you again, Brody. It's been awhile."

"You too, Ryder." Brody smiled at another of his old friends. Ryder Wolfe owned a lucrative American Paint horse ranch. He'd been one of Brody's childhood friends, along with the Stone brothers, Riley Madison, Trick Dillon, and of course, Sam.

"Brody? It's good to see you again." Wyatt Stone stuck his hand out as he elbowed Ryder out of the way and shook Brody's hand.

"Damn, Wyatt, you're still as ugly as ever."

Wyatt grinned. "Jealous?"

"Hell yes. Between you, Sam, and Trick, the

rest of us were rebounds."

Olivia snickered. Brody watched as Wyatt narrowed his eyes at her. "Did you say something?"

Brody watched as she fluttered her eyelashes at him. Wyatt's jaw clenched and he gave Brody a nod and stalked away. Brody glanced at Jake and Gabe. They were both grinning. He shook his head. "He doesn't have a snowball's chance in hell." He turned to Ryder. "Do you and Wyatt have a problem with each other?"

Ryder chuckled. "Only that he thinks Olivia and I are an item." Ryder shook his head. "We're just friends. Hell, if Wyatt wants her, I'm not standing in the way. I just don't know what his problem with her is."

Brody smiled at Ryder and then Olivia. "Like I said, snowball's chance in hell."

Olivia grinned at him. "Okay, now you can call me Liv." Then she, Becca, and Emma moved back toward the table to help serve the people eating.

Trick Dillon strode toward him and stuck out a hand. "Brody, it's been way too long."

Brody smiled at him. "I see you haven't aged well at all, Dillon." He laughed since it was far from the truth. Trick Dillon was as tall as he was, with black hair and black eyes. He demanded attention anywhere he went. Women loved him but his heart belonged to his wife, Kaylee.

Trick grinned at him. "I feel like I haven't some days, that's for sure."

"Where's Kaylee?" Brody glanced around.

Trick peered over his shoulder. "In the

kitchen, I think. You know how she is. She'd do all the cleaning up if we'd let her."

As they talked, a beautiful woman with blonde hair and dark green eyes strolled up to them and slipped her arm through Trick's arm. She smiled at both men.

"It's good to see you, Brody," Kaylee Dillon said.

"You still look amazing, Kaylee." Brody chuckled when she blushed. "I still don't understand why you're with this ugly guy." He jerked his head toward Trick.

"I felt sorry for him. No one else wanted him." Kaylee laughed softly when Trick growled at her.

"I'm glad no one else wanted me." Trick chuckled.

"We need to get going. You have a client coming later this afternoon, Patrick."

"I know. Let's go say our goodbyes." He stuck his hand out to Brody again. "Don't be a stranger. Come out to the ranch sometime. We'll all go for a ride."

"Sounds good." Brody shook Trick's hand and kissed Kaylee on her cheek. He watched them walk away together and leave.

Brody smiled when he saw Madilyn and Kaitlyn enter the room. Kaitlyn stood by Sam and their parents. Madilyn headed toward Brody.

"Hi, Jake, Gabe." She smiled.

"Madilyn. How's Katie?" Gabe asked.

Madilyn shrugged. "She's fine. I don't think she loved him anymore anyway."

"Who could love that prick?" Gabe muttered. "He treated Katie like dirt and she's the sweetest woman around."

Brody agreed. Since he'd been friends with Sam growing up, he knew Katie very well. "I remember Sam telling me about her getting married. I was invited to the wedding but I was on assignment and couldn't make it. Sam didn't want her to marry him, but there wasn't anything he could do about it. I don't even think their parents approved of Parker. But Katie was in love."

"I know. I attended the wedding and Sam scowled the entire day," Madilyn told them.

Brody shrugged. "Sam has great instincts about people."

"Well, he was certainly right about Parker," Jake said. "I wonder what she'll do now."

Madilyn's eyes met Brody's. He shook his head. "Who knows? She still has her job at the shop but I don't think she makes enough to make the house payments." Brody shrugged. "I wonder if Parker had life insurance."

Jake grunted. "If he did, who was the beneficiary?"

Brody saw Madilyn frown. "Katie never mentioned it so I doubt it."

Everyone fell silent with their own thoughts. Brody glanced over to see Katie still standing beside Sam as people started leaving and giving their condolences. Jake and Gabe strolled away to gather up their wives and hug Kaitlyn before they left. Eventually, the only guests left were Madilyn and Brody.

"I'd better go. I don't want Sam knowing I know anything about this. He'd be pissed I know before he does," Brody whispered to Madilyn.

"All right. I'll walk you out."

Brody hugged Kaitlyn, shook Sam's hand, and then hugged their parents. "I'll see you tomorrow, Sam. Katie, if you need anything, please don't hesitate to ask."

Kaitlyn smiled at him. "Thank you, Brody."

"I'll be right back," Madilyn told her. "I'm going to walk Brody out."

They walked out to Brody's truck. He pulled her into his arms and pressed his lips to hers. His lips moved across her cheek to her neck. "Come to the house after you leave here."

"All right. I'll be there as soon as I can. I'll have to go home and pick up some clothes to change into."

He kissed her quickly. "Good luck in there." He gave her a grin, hopped into his truck and pulled out.

Chapter Seven

Madilyn headed back inside and started cleaning up. Kaitlyn began to help her when Sam stopped her.

"I'll help, Madilyn. You go sit down, Katie."

"I'm not an invalid, Sam. I can help. Then I want to talk to you all about something."

Madilyn saw Sam and their parents frown but Sam nodded. "All right." They left the room.

Kaitlyn's hands were shaking. Madilyn took them in hers. "Are you all right?"

"I'm scared to death to tell them," Kaitlyn whispered.

Madilyn sighed. "I know, but you have to tell them. Maybe you don't need to tell them about the rape."

Kaitlyn laughed. "I'd rather tell them the truth and get it out there and Sam's going to know I wouldn't sleep with a man I knew was screwing around on me." She sighed. "Let's get this over with."

They entered the living room to find Sam lying on the sofa with his eyes closed. Their parents sat in the recliners. Kaitlyn moved toward Sam. His eyes flew open.

"Were you sleeping?" Kaitlyn asked softly.

"Just resting my eyes," Sam said as he sat up. "What did you want to talk about?"

Kaitlyn sat in a wingback chair and Madilyn sat in a rocking chair. Her stomach was in knots.

She couldn't imagine how Kaitlyn's was. Madilyn watched her take a deep breath and Sam narrowed his eyes. Kaitlyn cleared her throat.

"I'm pregnant," she said softly.

"What?" Sam asked between clenched teeth.

Kaitlyn nodded. "I'm two months pregnant."

"You slept with that cheating son of a bitch, when you knew he was fucking around on you?"

"Sam!" their mother chastised him.

"Not intentionally," Kaitlyn whispered.

"Not intentionally? What the hell do you mean by that, Kaitlyn?" Sam asked quietly.

Madilyn reached over, grabbed Kaitlyn's hand, and gave it a squeeze. She gave her a small nod when Kaitlyn glanced at her.

"Kevin...raped me."

Madilyn watched as Sam tried to get his emotions under control, his hands clenched and unclenched. "He what?"

"Sam—" Madilyn stopped when he glared at her. Kaitlyn's parents hadn't said a word or reacted in any way.

"He was drunk one night, and I was accusing him of sleeping with Beth. He said if I was more of a wife, he wouldn't have to screw around." Kaitlyn's voice caught. "I said it didn't matter anymore since I would never sleep with him again. It set him off. He took me to the bedroom and raped me."

"Why didn't you tell me? Rape is rape." Sam stood and moved to squat down in front of her.

"Because you'd have killed him."

"I wouldn't have killed him. I would have beat the shit out of him then arrested him."

"I don't know what I'm going to do, Sam. I want this baby, even though it wasn't made in love, but I don't know how I can afford it."

"You can come here and live. I'll take care of you. Isn't that what big brothers do? Take care of their baby sisters?"

"You can always come home with us, Katie." These were the first words Kaitlyn's father had uttered.

Madilyn stood. "I'm going to go and let you all talk. I'll see you whenever you get back to work, Katie. Take your time. I can run the shop."

"I'll be in tomorrow."

"Katie, you just buried your husband," Madilyn said.

"A husband who cheated on me and raped me. I'm glad he's gone. I'll be in tomorrow."

Madilyn glanced at Sam. He shrugged. Madilyn smiled. "All right. I'll see you tomorrow, but if you change your mind, it's no problem."

"I won't change my mind. I'll see you tomorrow," Kaitlyn said with conviction.

Madilyn nodded and left. She knew once Kaitlyn made up her mind there wasn't anything that she could do to change it. Maybe it was better she did return to work, rather than sit around and think. Madilyn couldn't imagine what she was going through. Pregnant by a man who'd raped her and obviously didn't love her, a job that barely paid enough to support her, and now she would have a child to care for. Madilyn would do anything she could to help but she had her own bills to take care of. She shook her head as she drove home to change and then go to

Brody's place. She wanted to be with him, and spend the rest of her life with him, if he wanted her. After getting what she needed from her apartment, she drove to Brody's ranch. He came out on the porch to meet her. She watched as he leaned against a post, folded his arms, and crossed his booted feet. He grinned at her and her heart hit her stomach. He was so gorgeous. Stepping from the car, she leaned back against it, folded her arms, and smiled up at him.

"Hi," she said softly.

"How did it go with Sam? I'm sure their parents were supportive, but Sam..."

"He was livid but supportive. He told Katie she could stay there with him, but I know she doesn't want to invade his space. I think Sam would kill Kevin if he wasn't dead already. Her parents said she could live with them, but I can't see that happening. Katie isn't going to want to live with her parents in San Diego. I really can't see her leaving Clifton."

"I agree, and you're right, Sam would kill him. He adores Katie and he'd do anything for her." Brody walked down the steps then stopped in front of her. "Hi." Then he pulled her into his arms and kissed her. Madilyn moaned against his lips. His tongue moved slowly into her mouth as he pulled her tighter against him. Brody groaned as he deepened the kiss. He pulled back slowly and stared into her eyes. "I love you, Maddie. I always have and I always will."

"Oh, Brody. I love you too. So much." Madilyn wrapped her arms around his neck.

"Marry me," Brody whispered against her

neck.

"Are you serious?"

"Yes, of course."

"Are you staying here in Clifton?" Madilyn stared into his eyes.

Brody glanced away from her and sighed. "Yes. I want to start the ranch back up. Mom and Dad are all for it. I'll still be a deputy, Maddie. You'll have to accept it."

"I do, Brody. I don't care where you go, I'm going with you."

"Move in here until we can get a date set."

"I'd like to keep my apartment. It's close to work."

"All right but on Saturday nights you'd better be here."

Madilyn squealed and kissed him. Brody laughed and picked her up and carried her inside the house and to the bedroom. He laid her on the bed and came down beside her. Madilyn took his glasses off and placed them on the nightstand then reached for him. She pushed him to his back, straddled him, and ran her hands up under his t-shirt, over his six pack and up to his pecs. His skin quivered under her fingers. She leaned down to kiss him, took his bottom lip between her teeth, and sucked it into her mouth. Brody growled low in his throat. His hands ran up her back and into her hair. Madilyn sat up and removed her shirt then her bra. She scooched down his legs, unsnapped his jeans, and slowly lowered the zipper. Her hand snaked inside and wrapped around him. His hips lifted and he pushed his jeans off.

Madilyn grinned and crawled to the end of the bed and pulled his boots off, then his jeans. She slowly moved up his body, kissing his calves, then to his thighs. He hissed in a breath when she lowered his boxer briefs and ran her tongue along the length of him. His hands clenched in her hair. She moved her mouth down over him, taking him deep into her mouth, and sucked. Brody groaned deep in his throat. Madilyn ran her tongue around the tip and down the length. His hips jerked.

"Maddie, stop please," he moaned.

"Nope." She continued to drive him wild until he jack-knifed up and grabbed her. Brody tossed her to her back, rolled on a condom and moved between her legs. He took her lips in a deep kiss and slowly inched into her. Madilyn gasped as he filled her. She wrapped her arms around his neck and her legs around his waist and held on while he moved harder and faster against her.

"Maddie, come with me," he whispered against her lips.

"Yes..." she moaned and cried out his name.

Brody growled her name out as he joined her tumbling over the edge. After catching their breaths, he rolled to his back and pulled her tight against him. They fell asleep in each other's arms.

* * * *

A few hours later, Madilyn silently crept around the room looking for her clothes when the lamp beside the bed came on. She jumped and glanced at Brody.

"Sneaking out on me? I feel so cheap," Brody

said as he sat up against the headboard.

"I didn't mean to wake you. I have to get going." She put her knee on the bed, leaned down, and kissed him. "Call me tomorrow."

"I will. I'm starting back on my regular shift tomorrow night but I'm off from Saturday to Monday night." Brody tried to pull her into the bed.

Madilyn laughed. "Stop. I have to go." She quickly kissed him. "I love you."

"I love you, too. Be careful driving Copper Ridge."

Madilyn blew him a kiss and ran out the door. She hated driving in the dark but she couldn't stay. Not tonight. In two nights, she'd go stay with him for the weekend. She grinned. Being back with him was amazing. It was as if no time had passed and they'd never been apart. Madilyn frowned as it started to rain. Driving in the dark was bad enough, but add in rain and it was almost impossible. The headlights reflected off the wet road. She slowly drove the curve of Copper Ridge. A car came up behind her and was too close for her liking, staying close to her bumper. There was no place to pull over and let them pass so she lightly tapped her brakes. The car fell back from her. She breathed a sigh of relief and finally made it to her apartment complex. When she pulled in, the car slowed and for a minute she thought it was going to pull in behind her but it picked up speed and drove on past.

She blew out a relieved breath. She certainly wasn't in the mood for any confrontation. Pulling into her parking spot, Madilyn locked her car and ran for the overhang to get out of the rain. A scream tore from her when a dark figure stepped in front of her. A hand covered her mouth.

"Shut up." *Zach!*

Madilyn kicked his shin and scratched at his face. "Get away from me," she shouted.

Zach pulled her up the stairs to her apartment and shoved her to her door. "Open it," he growled.

"Go to hell," Madilyn screamed.

Zach wrestled her keys from her hand and unlocked her door. Once opened, he pushed her inside. Madilyn ran for the phone but Zach tackled her and rolled her to her back. She fought back and started to scream again but he put his hand over her mouth.

"Shut up, Madilyn. I'm not going to hurt you."

She stopped struggling and nodded. He removed his hand and stood. Madilyn kicked her foot up into his groin and watched as he fell to his knees. She scrambled up, grabbed the phone, and called the sheriff's department. Then she ran behind the sofa and kept an eye on Zach. He laid on the floor groaning. Since the sheriff's department was just down the street, they were there in minutes.

Madilyn opened the door to Deputy Mark Shaw. "Come in, Mark."

"Madilyn? Did you call us?"

She moved aside to show him Zach lying on the floor. "Yes. He attacked me."

"Are you hurt?" Mark glanced at her as he strolled over to Zach and squatted down.

"I'm fine. He scared me. I kicked him in his family jewels." She folded her arms across her chest and sniffed.

"Get up, Johnson," Mark told Zach.

"I can't yet," Zach groaned.

Madilyn watched as Mark grabbed Zach by the back of his collar and lifted him from the floor. "I don't care if you can or not. You're going in." He glanced at Madilyn. "You are pressing charges, right?"

"This time, I am."

"This time?" Mark's eyebrow rose.

Madilyn waved her hand. "Never mind. It's a long story, but yes, I'm pressing charges."

Mark handcuffed Zach and had him sit on the couch. He took a pad out of his shirt pocket. "Tell me what happened tonight."

"I was running from my car and he grabbed me. Then he dragged me up here, took my keys, and then pushed me into my apartment. I tried to run for the phone and he tackled me. That's when I kicked him."

Mark nodded. "Good enough." He pulled Zach up from the sofa and led him from the apartment. Madilyn could hear him reading Zach his rights. She moved to her couch and collapsed on it. What had he been planning to do? She shivered. Was he going to force himself on her? Leaning her head back against the sofa, she closed her eyes. If Brody found out about this, there would be hell to pay. He'd kill Zach. Madilyn sat up and reached for her phone and dialed Sam's number.

"Garrett," he answered.

"Sam, it's Madilyn."

"Is something wrong?" She could hear the concern in his voice.

"I shouldn't have called…"

"Madilyn, tell me."

She sighed and told Sam what happened with Zach and Mark arresting him. "I'm afraid when Brody finds out, he'll go ballistic."

"That's putting it mildly," Sam muttered. "I'll talk to him tomorrow when he goes in for his shift. I'll take care of it."

"Thank you. Is Katie all right?"

"She's fine. Sound asleep. It's been a rough day for her."

"I'll let you go, Sam. Thank you." She heard him hang up.

Madilyn stood and headed for her bathroom. She hoped a hot shower would help her relax and help her forget what almost happened.

* * * *

Wilson Delgado sat in his car and watched as the sheriff's deputy put a man in the back of the patrol car and then pulled out of the parking lot. Wilson wasn't sure which apartment the man was taken from but he really didn't care either. He was there to keep an eye on Madilyn Young and get her routine down so he could make his move. He grinned as he thought of how Morgan would panic when he took her from his life.

Wilson turned on the wipers to clear the windshield. The rain was coming down heavier, making it almost impossible to see. He sighed and started the car. There wasn't much he was going to see tonight. He doubted she would leave her apartment anymore tonight since she'd just gotten home from Morgan's. Wilson followed her from Morgan's ranch and drove on past when she pulled into her parking lot. He circled back and parked. It would have been so easy to run her off the road but that would have been too simple. Morgan needed to suffer for what he'd done to Abby. For what he'd made Wilson do to his wife. His fist hit the steering wheel. The lying whore. She swore she wasn't seeing anyone but he'd had her followed. When he saw the pictures, he saw red and put his plan into action. Wilson grunted as he remembered the night he'd had her killed.

"Wilson, please. Please don't do this." Abby begged while she grabbed the lapels of his jacket.

"Get off me, you fucking whore. Do you think you can lie to me?" he yelled.

"I'm not lying. We only had lunch together a few times."

Wilson slapped her and shoved her to the ground. He strode away from her to his car and opened the glove box. When he came back to her, he shoved the glossy photos in her face while he grabbed her hair. He put his face next to hers.

"Pictures don't lie, bitch!" He pushed her to the ground and turned to the two men standing by the car. "Kill her, get rid of the body."

"Wilson," she screamed.

He stood over her. "No one, especially my wife, lies to me." He strode to the car. "Kill her," he growled as he stood beside his car and watched them shoot his wife. Wilson knew her body wouldn't be found for a long time. Cheyenne,

Wyoming was a long way from Butte, Montana. With any luck, animals would ravage it. Knowing his men would do as instructed, Wilson drove back to Butte. The bitch deserved what she got, but Morgan would pay, too. The thought of taking someone from him kept Wilson going. He would take care of this one himself then head into Canada. With more than enough money to live on, he'd disappear.

What a whore his wife turned out to be. He was glad she was dead but he didn't understand why she whored around. Wilson gave her everything she wanted. Cars, jewelry, clothes, and a huge home to live in. He hit his fist on the steering wheel again. *Bitch!* He was better off without her. Revenge was going to taste so sweet when he took Madilyn Young away from Brody Morgan.

* * * *

Brody jerked awake and sat up. The dreams were back. Nightmares were more like it. He kept seeing Abby lying in a shallow grave, the animals digging at the dirt and pulling her out. Only, she wasn't dead. Her screams woke him for months after she'd been found. *Jesus!* He ran his hand down his face and took deep breaths. Why now? Her death was over a year ago. He'd been free of the nightmares for months now.

Brody swung his legs off the bed and headed toward the kitchen. It was almost dawn. Getting a glass of water, he leaned against the countertop and gazed out at the sun coming over the mountains. The sky was beautiful with pink, blue, and yellow hues. He glanced over to the old hay barn. It was time to tear it down and build a new one. The ranch prospered in its day. Black Angus cattle had roamed the pastures. Brody wanted to make a go of it again. He knew he could do it and he wanted Madilyn alongside him. Their kids running around the fields and barns as he'd done growing up. Both red barns needed repainting. He'd take care of that too.

Damn it! Why did he have the dream? He made coffee and headed for the shower while it brewed. Today, he'd start on tearing down the barn and sleep later. Back to work tonight. He really hated nightshift.

* * * *

Madilyn sat at the counter placing orders for the shop when Kaitlyn strolled through the door. True to her word, she showed up for work. Madilyn smiled at her.

"Are you sure you want to be here?" she asked.

"No place else I'd rather be. I have bills to pay." Kaitlyn smiled at her. "I'm going to the house tonight and get some things. I'm going to stay with Sam until I can get an apartment."

Madilyn grinned. "He talked you into it, huh?"

Kaitlyn laughed. "What can I say? My big brother is very persuasive."

Madilyn moved around the counter and hugged her. "I'm glad. Are you going to sell the house?"

"Yes. There is nothing but bad memories there. I want to start over with my baby."

Madilyn nodded at her. "It'll be a good start."

Later in the afternoon, as Madilyn sat at the

counter, the bell rang above the door announcing a customer. She automatically smiled at them. The man headed straight for her. No smile touched his lips.

"Could you get Kaitlyn Parker for me?" he asked.

"Yes, sir, I certainly can." Madilyn headed for the back office and knocked. Kaitlyn told her to enter. "There's a man at the counter asking for you."

Kaitlyn frowned up at her and stood. They walked together to the front of the shop.

"Mr. Scott?" Kaitlyn asked in a surprised voice. "What can I do for you?"

Cal Scott was the owner of the Clifton Florist and Greenhouse. Why he was there was anyone's guess. In the five years Madilyn worked there, she'd never met him until today.

"Katie, first off let me say I'm sorry for your loss. I went to your home first but when you weren't there, I called Sam. I couldn't believe it when he said you were working." He took a deep breath. "Secondly, I'm selling the shop. Millie and I want to travel. Visit our children. I'm sorry to spring this on you but as of tomorrow it will go up for sale. I am stipulating you and Miz Young be allowed to remain here if the person buying it keeps it as it is." He shrugged. "If they change it to some other type of business, I'm afraid you'll both be out of jobs and I have no control over that."

Madilyn didn't know what to say and she knew Kaitlyn felt the same way. If they lost their jobs, they were both in trouble. Jobs were scarce in Clifton, even with the B and B doing so well, it was only open five months out of the year. She had no idea what would happen if it came down to the shop closing.

"I'm sorry to tell you this the day after you buried your husband, but Millie and I are leaving on a cruise tomorrow and I wanted to tell you in person. I know how much you love working here and I really hope the new owner will keep it as it is," Cal Scott said.

"I understand, Mr. Scott," Kaitlyn said softly.

He nodded and left, leaving Madilyn and Kaitlyn staring at the door he'd disappeared through. Kaitlyn sighed and took a seat behind the counter. Madilyn leaned against it.

"I can't believe this," Kaitlyn whispered. "As if I don't have enough to deal with, now I have to deal with the possibility of losing my job."

"I'm sorry, Katie."

"Oh, Madilyn. I didn't mean to sound selfish. I know you're worried too."

"I am, but you have a baby to think of."

"Maybe I should have an abortion." Kaitlyn's voice caught on a sob.

"No! You know you can't do that. You'd never be able to live with yourself."

"You're right. I'll manage somehow."

Both women were lost in their own thoughts then finally got back to work. The thought of losing her job stayed in the back of Madilyn's mind all through the rest of the day. She was sure Kaitlyn was going through the same thing. Kaitlyn had Sam to help her, though. Madilyn wasn't sure how Brody would feel about it. He'd asked her to marry him but nowadays, both people in a marriage held jobs. Being married to Brody, Madilyn knew she wouldn't need to work but she'd want to. At least, until she had children.

Madilyn took her break, called Brody, and hoped she didn't wake him up. Since he was going back to work tonight, he may be asleep.

"Hey, baby," he said in way of answering.

"Hi." Madilyn chewed on her bottom lip.

"What's wrong, Maddie?"

"The owner of the shop came in today to let us know he's putting it on the market tomorrow. He's going to stipulate we keep our jobs as long as it's kept as a florist and greenhouse but if the new owner changes it to something else, we could be out of jobs."

"Aww, baby. I'm sorry. I know how much you love it there. What do you need me to do?"

Madilyn blinked back tears at the concern in his voice. "Just be there for me."

"Always. You know, if you lose your job, you'll have to move in with me."

She could hear the smile in his voice. "Yes, I know." She sighed.

Brody's chuckle came over the line. "We could get married right away then you'd have to move here anyway."

"You've got it all figured out, don't you, Brody?"

"Seriously, we can get married whenever you want. Tomorrow sounds good to me."

"I'd love to, but let's see what happens first, okay?" she whispered.

"Whatever you want, Maddie." Brody sighed. "I have so much to do out here and I'd hate to have you move in yet anyway. I want to knock down the old hay barn and build a new one. I want to build it myself though."

"You need to have a 'barn raising'. The people of Clifton would help you build it."

"They still do that here?" Brody sounded surprised.

Madilyn laughed. "Yes, of course. This is Clifton, remember?"

"I'll put a post on the bulletin board at the feed store tonight."

"You'll get a lot of help. I'll get with the women to make food. Just let me know when you want to do it."

"All right. I'd like that." Brody sighed. "I'm here anytime, Maddie."

"I know, Brody. I'd better go. I love you."

"I love you more." He hung up.

Madilyn smiled and headed out to the greenhouse. Brody was right. She loved this job and it would hurt to lose it but she was also a firm believer in everything happened for a reason. She may not know the reasons yet but she hoped that one day it would all become clear.

Chapter Eight

Brody drove to the station and walked inside. He was surprised to see Sam still there. He leaned against the doorjamb and folded his arms.

"Do you go home anymore, Sam?" Brody grinned.

"It sure as hell doesn't feel like it. Mark isn't coming in, so you're on your own. I'll stay for a while but I don't like leaving Katie alone too long."

"Is she doing all right? Maddie said she worked today."

"She did. Seems she doesn't care about burying her cheating husband yesterday."

Brody snorted. "No one cared about him. She's better off without him."

Sam stood and strolled around the desk. "I know. I'm glad she's free of him now and especially after what I found out about the bastard."

"Raping her?" Brody said softly.

"Did Madilyn tell you?" Sam leaned back against his desk and folded his arms.

"Yes. I'm sorry Katie went through it, but she'll love the baby unconditionally."

Sam straightened up. "Of course. I'll go to Dewey's with you, and then I'm heading home."

Brody and Sam walked out, got into the Sheriff's SUV, and drove to Dewey's bar. They strolled inside to hear loud music blaring and the place wall-to-wall people.

"Is this place always packed?" Brody yelled above the music.

"Every night of the week." Sam jerked his chin. "Head off that way, I'll go this way."

They managed to make the rounds without incident. As they drove back to the station, Brody glanced over to Sam. "Did Katie mention the sale of the shop?"

"Yes," Sam growled. "She loves the place. I don't know what she'll do if she can't work there."

"Maddie's pretty upset too. There aren't too many jobs in this town."

"You got that shit right. Katie mentioned moving away. I don't want her to do that. She's all I have here as far as family. With our parents living in San Diego, we're all we have."

Brody didn't say anything. He knew how Sam felt since his own parents were traveling all the time but he'd gotten used to being alone while he lived in Butte. When they pulled into the station, Brody hopped out and Sam left. Brody didn't like being on nightshift as it was, but to be on it alone was a little intimidating. He agreed with Sam's idea of two deputies together at all times. It was just safer. No one for backup wasn't a smart move. Brody knew if there was trouble, though, all he had to do was call Sam and he'd be there.

Brody sat at his desk working on reports when he heard the front door open and then listened as footsteps came toward his office. He stood up and put his hand on his weapon, unsnapping the holster. He breathed a sigh of relief when he saw

Madilyn stop in the doorway. She grinned at him.

"Hello, deputy."

Brody pursed his lips. "What can I do for you, Miz Young?"

She laughed softly. "Loaded question, deputy." She glanced around. "Are you here alone?"

"Yeah. Mark didn't come in tonight. Sam didn't say why." He moved around the desk and stopped in front of her. "What are you doing here?"

"I just wanted to see you. Is that a problem...deputy?"

Brody watched her roll her lips in to keep from smiling. "I don't have a problem with it at all." He took her hand, pulled her into the office, closed the door behind her, and pushed her back against it. He pressed his lips to hers. When she moaned, he deepened the kiss and slowly moved his tongue into her mouth. Her hands wrapped around his neck. Brody picked her up and carried her to the sofa. He sat down with her straddling his lap, never taking his lips from hers. He groaned when she took her lips from his.

"I didn't come over here for this, Brody."

"Maybe not, but since you're here..." He moved his mouth to her neck.

Madilyn pushed away from him and stood. Brody stared up at her. "I want to get married."

Brody grinned at her. "I do too, baby."

"No. I mean now."

"It's too late tonight."

"Must you be such a smartass?" She put her

hands on her hips and glared at him.

Brody chuckled. "I already told you, we can get married whenever you want. However you want."

"What if I lose my job?"

Brody stood and took her in his arms. "Have you forgotten I come from a rich family? My parents gave me the ranch and I want to get it to a working ranch again. Eventually, I may stop working in law enforcement."

"Really?"

"If I can make a go of the ranch, then yes. And I don't see a problem getting it back on its feet. Morgan beef was the best out there. I can get the reputation back again." Brody ran his hands up and down her arms.

"You didn't think this way before."

"I've been thinking about it a lot lately. I loved working the ranch, though at times, I didn't think that way. I was young and wanted to do anything but work it. I'm sure I can make a go of it."

"I don't know about just sitting around the house all day," Madilyn whispered.

"You'd have enough to do taking care of our kids."

Madilyn grinned at him. "Do you plan on keeping me barefoot and pregnant?"

"I plan on practicing to keep you barefoot and pregnant." Brody chuckled when she blushed.

Madilyn stepped back from him and placed her hands on her slim hips. "You think you're so funny."

Brody pulled her to him. "You think I'm funny,

too." He nuzzled her neck.

They sprang apart when they heard the front door open. Brody opened his office door and stepped out. Joe Baker stood in the lobby glancing around. Brody sighed and walked toward him.

"What can I do for you?"

Joe Baker glared at Brody. "Where's Garrett?" The man could barely stand.

"He's not here. What do you want?" Brody put his hands on his hips and narrowed his eyes at Baker.

"I want to tell that son of a bitch not to come out to my property again," Baker slurred.

"I'm sure the sheriff will only go there if he needs to. Did you drive here?"

"Of course I drove here. How the hell else would I get here?"

"You're drunk and shouldn't be driving."

"I ain't in my truck so you can't arrest me." Baker grinned.

Brody smirked. "Not yet. How do you plan on getting home?"

Baker's eyes widened. "You can't do that."

"I can and I will. Now, you have two choices. You either get in the cell and sleep it off or you leave, and once you get inside your truck, I'll arrest you. Either way, you'll be in the cell tonight."

"I ain't going in no cell," Baker shouted.

"One way or another, you are." Brody stepped closer toward him.

Baker spun around and headed out the door. Brody followed and watched as Baker tried to climb into his truck. The minute he got behind the wheel and started the truck, Brody yanked him out of it and handcuffed him then dragged him back into the station. He pulled him to the cell and shoved him inside it. Baker started ranting the second the door clanged shut.

"You let me out of here, you son of a bitch," he yelled.

"Shut up," Brody said quietly. He glanced toward his office when he saw Madilyn coming out of it. He swore under his breath, hating that she witnessed it. She walked toward him and stopped in front of him. He raised his eyebrows when she grinned at him.

"That was really hot."

Brody stared at her a few seconds then burst out laughing. He pulled her into his arms and kissed her hard and quick. "I aim to please, ma'am."

Madilyn laughed. "You do it well, deputy." She shook her head. "Who would think I'd think it was sexy the way you arrested him?"

Brody chuckled. "It's the uniform."

"Uniform? You only wear a khaki shirt with a badge...oh, maybe it is the uniform." She squealed when he picked her up, carried her to his office, and kicked the door shut.

His lips captured hers in a deep kiss. He trailed his mouth across her cheek to her ear, taking the lobe into his mouth. He grinned when he felt her shiver. Brody stepped back when she pushed at his chest.

"We are not having sex in your office, Brody," Madilyn scolded.

Brody laughed. "Spoilsport."

Madilyn walked around him. "I have to get home. I'll talk to you later."

"Hold on. I'll take you home." He picked up the keys to the cruiser and followed her out the door. The moon was beginning to make an appearance and stars were already starting to wink against the darkening sky. Brody opened the door for her then walked around the cruiser and got in. He glanced over at her.

"I wish I could go home with you and crawl into bed."

"I wish you could, too. You really didn't have to drive me home. It's just across the street."

"It's getting dark and I don't want you alone out here. What kind of lawman would I be if I let you walk home?"

Madilyn chuckled. "That's true but you left a prisoner in the jail and no one to watch him."

"Shhh. Don't tell anyone. It'll only take a minute then I'll get back to the office." He pulled into the parking lot, turned the car off, and turned toward her. "Come here."

Madilyn smiled and tried to get closer to him but with a computer and a shotgun between them, it wasn't easy. She leaned toward him and kissed him then smiled at him, got out, and ran to her apartment. Brody got out and ran after her. He grasped her arm.

"Wait. Let me walk you up."

"I do this all the time, Brody," she scolded.

"I'm not going anywhere until I see you safe in your apartment."

Madilyn shook her head. "You've lived in the

big city too long. This is Clifton. Nothing happens here."

Brody growled. "I'm walking you up. Damn that hardheaded." He walked her to her door and waited while she unlocked it, then he pulled her into his arms and kissed her. "I'll call you tomorrow. I love you." He turned and ran down the stairs.

Brody drove back to the station and strolled through the door. He came to a stop when he heard Joe Baker snoring. Laughing softly, he headed for his office and did some paperwork. It was going to be a long night.

* * * *

Madilyn entered her bathroom to relax in the tub before going to bed. After pouring bubble bath under the running water, she pinned her hair on top of her head and was about to get in when her home phone rang. Sighing, she ran to her bedroom to get it. The number showed up as 'Private.'

"Hello?" she answered.

"Is this Madilyn Young?" a male voice asked.

"Yes, who's this?"

"You don't know me, Miz Young. Not yet anyway. But you will." He laughed.

Madilyn shivered. "What do you mean?"

The man chuckled. "I mean, you and I are going to become good friends, Madilyn. We have a friend in common. Brody Morgan."

Madilyn breathed a sigh of relief. It was a friend of Brody's. "I see. Did he have you call me for some reason? Is everything all right?"

"Everything is fine...for now and no, he didn't

have me call you. I took that upon myself. You see, I want to get to know the woman who has Morgan's heart in the palm of her hand."

A bad feeling swept over Madilyn. "Why?" she whispered.

"Because he got to know my wife before she was killed and I want the same courtesy."

Madilyn gasped and hung up. She started shaking as she sat on the bed. Dear God. Should she call Brody? No. He'd come to her and he had to stay at the station. Grabbing her robe, she put it on, slowly moved toward the window in her living room, and quickly closed the blinds. After making certain she'd locked the door and set the deadbolt, she moved back to the bathroom and quickly bathed. She crawled into bed and pulled the blanket up to her chin. Wilson Delgado was letting her know he wanted revenge and he'd use her to get it. She was scared and wanted to call Brody but she couldn't. There was no one to cover for him and he needed to be on the job. Madilyn knew morning couldn't come soon enough and she could talk to Brody about the phone call. It was going to be a sleepless night.

* * * *

At six thirty the next morning, Madilyn strolled into the sheriff's department. She smiled at Betty Lou.

"I need to talk to Brody."

"He's in Sam's office. I'll let them know you're here."

"Thank you, Betty Lou—"

"Sam," Betty Lou shouted.

Sam came striding out of his office. "Why can't

you use the damn intercom?"

"Don't you swear at me, Sam Garrett," Betty Lou huffed.

Madilyn heard Sam sigh. "Sam, can I talk to you and Brody?" She saw the surprise on his face.

"I didn't see you, Madilyn. Of course. Come on back." He led her to his office. Brody stood when she entered the room.

"Maddie? Are you all right? You look tired."

"I didn't sleep much." She took a seat across from Sam's desk. Brody and Sam both sat.

"What is it?" Sam asked.

"I think Wilson Delgado called me last night."

"*What?*" Brody jumped up. "What do you mean, 'you think'?"

"A man called me and told me we had a friend in common." She glanced at Brody. "You. Then he said he wanted to get to know me since you knew his wife before she was killed and he wanted the same courtesy." Her voice caught on a sob.

"That son of a bitch. He's here, Sam," Brody muttered. He gazed at Madilyn. "You're coming to the ranch to stay."

"What good is that going to do? I still have to come into town for work," Madilyn reminded him.

Brody didn't take his eyes off her. "Tell her, Sam."

Madilyn glanced at Sam to see him nod. "He's right, Madilyn. We can't give him any opportunity to get to you."

"I'll be alone out there at night. Isn't that

worse?"

Brody sat back down. "Shit," he growled. "She's right."

"Then I'll move you to day shift. At least at night, you'll be together and during the day, you'll both be working," Sam told them.

"How are we going to do that? Rick will pitch a fit working nights," Brody said.

"He'll do what I tell him to do." Sam picked up the phone and called Rick into his office.

When Rick strolled in, he smiled at Madilyn and Brody. "What's up, Sam?"

"I'm switching you to nights for a while." Sam raised his hand when Rick started to interrupt. "Hopefully it won't be for long, but I need you to do this, Rick. No questions asked."

"All right, Sam. You're the boss." Rick gave him a nod.

"Go home, Brody. I'll see you tomorrow. Rick you can start tomorrow night."

Madilyn, Brody, and Rick left Sam's office. Brody glanced at Rick. "I appreciate it, Rick."

"No problem, Brody. I'm not sure what's going on, but I'll help however I can," he told Brody.

Brody put his hand out to him. "I appreciate it, Rick. Hopefully, it won't be too long for you."

Rick shook his hand and then entered his office. Brody and Madilyn walked outside. The summer heat slapped them in the face. The thought of being in the greenhouse today didn't sit well with Madilyn. It was bad enough on fall and spring days but in the stifling heat of August, it was a killer.

"I guess you have to work today." Brody

grinned at her.

"Yes. I don't want Katie alone too much right now." Madilyn smiled. "What did you have in mind?"

Brody pulled her close to him and whispered in her ear. "Horseback ride and then spend the day in bed."

Madilyn groaned. "I wish I could." She sighed. "Can you come back into town later to help me pack some clothes?"

Brody nodded. "Of course. I think I'll get started on tearing the old barn down since my plans to spend the day with you are shot to hell."

Madilyn laughed. "Sorry but I have a job...for now." She sobered, remembering it was possible she'd be out of a job soon. Sighing, she took his hand and started across the street toward the florist shop. It was early but she'd go ahead and open to get started on her day.

At the shop, she unlocked the doors and strolled in with Brody following her inside. She turned the alarm off then moved behind the counter. Brody stood in the middle of the shop, glancing around.

"What does he look like?" Madilyn asked.

Brody's mouth tightened. "I suppose women think he's good-looking. He's tall, around six foot, slim. Blonde hair, blue eyes. The son of a bitch is always tan. I think he has a damn tanning booth in that mansion of his."

Madilyn felt faint as she sat down. "I saw him."

"What?" Brody strode around the counter. "What do you mean you saw him? When?"

"A while back. A man came to my door asking

if Caroline was there. I told him he had the wrong apartment, it was a floor up. He smiled and left but he fits the description." She shivered. "I was confused, at first, because no one by that name lived upstairs but then I thought maybe he was just meeting her there." Madilyn raised tear filled eyes at him. "He was there to see me, wasn't he?"

Brody nodded. "He was scoping you and the apartment out." He swore. "Damn it." He ran his fingers through his hair. "I wonder how long he's been here. I wish you'd told me about this."

Madilyn placed her hands on her hips. "How was I supposed to know who he was? I thought he was just lost. You had no idea he was here."

"I know, but I should've known he'd show up. He's not the type to let something go. It doesn't matter how long ago it happened, he wants revenge. Revenge for something he did but blames me for." Brody paced. "I can't let you out of my sight."

"What are you going to do, Brody? Stay with me all day?"

"No. I know I can't do that, but I will come pick you up at the end of the day and take you to the ranch with me. Once there, you're not to leave my side." Brody strode toward her and cupped her face in his hands. "I won't let him get near you or I'll die trying to keep him from you."

Madilyn hugged him. She sighed when his arms tightened around her. This couldn't be over soon enough.

* * * *

At the end of the day, Madilyn stayed inside, waiting for Brody. Kaitlyn entered the front shop and smiled at her.

"I'm going to head home. I'll be late tomorrow. I have an appointment with an attorney first thing in the morning." Kaitlyn shook her head. "I have no idea what it's about, unless Kevin owed someone money or something. I'll be in as soon as the meeting is over."

"That's fine, Katie. Have you had any calls about the house?"

Kaitlyn nodded. "Yes. A family was by over the weekend. They really like it so I'm keeping my fingers crossed."

Madilyn smiled and watched as Kaitlyn left. Brody stopped her outside the shop to speak to her. Madilyn watched as Kaitlyn hugged him then headed for her car. Brody came inside and strolled up to her. He grinned at her and her heart hit her stomach.

"Ready to go home?" he said softly.

"Yes. It's been a long day." She moved around the counter and stood in front of him. "Why did Katie hug you?"

Brody chuckled. "Because I'm protecting you, she said."

Madilyn laughed. "She's priceless."

"Let's go. I don't want to be out after dark." Brody grasped her arm and led her from the store.

Madilyn locked the door and walked with Brody to his truck. She climbed up into it. "Could you have gotten a bigger truck?" she teased.

Brody laughed. "I don't think so. But, I am going to get a new bike as soon as I have a chance. I miss riding."

"I'd like to ride with you."

Brody glanced over to her. "You can *ride* with me anytime, baby."

Madilyn swatted her hand at him. "Stop."

His eyebrows went up. "What? What did I say?"

Madilyn snorted. "Men," she muttered.

Brody burst out laughing and started the truck. He drove them to the ranch and stopped by the back door. "I'm going to check the house. Stay here and lock the doors behind me. I'll only be a minute."

Madilyn nodded as he climbed out of the truck and strode into the house. Lights came on as he made his way through. She glanced around the yard. There were so many good memories here for her. A smile lifted her lips as she gazed at the huge red barn. They'd made love so many times in the hayloft. She chuckled as she remembered the time they'd almost been caught by Brody's dad. They lay in the hayloft trying not to laugh as Brody's dad walked through the barn yelling for them.

She was startled when Brody tapped on the window. Reaching over, she unlocked the door and climbed out. She couldn't keep the grin from her face.

"What are you grinning about?" Brody asked suspiciously.

"I was remembering when your dad almost caught us in the barn."

Brody laughed. "He may not have caught us but he knew when we walked into the house and you had hay in your hair."

Madilyn groaned. "I'd never been so embarrassed in my life as when he pulled it out of my hair."

Brody chuckled. "Mom had to look away. She was laughing so hard."

Madilyn slapped his arm. "It's not funny."

Brody pulled her against him and kissed her. "Yes, it is." He put her back to the truck and deepened the kiss. His tongue moved into her mouth and he groaned when she touched hers to his. "We need to go inside."

Madilyn nodded and took the hand he put out to her. They went inside and Brody locked the door behind them. She stood in the center of the kitchen and rubbed her arms. "I hate knowing he's out there. How does he know about me?"

Brody shrugged. "He has connections. He can find out anything he wants. I'm sure he's not here alone either. I'm sure he's brought his henchmen with him." Brody sighed. "It won't do any good to ask around about new people in town with all the tourists here."

Madilyn turned from him and headed toward the living room. She took a seat on the sofa. Brody joined her and took her hands in his. "We'll keep an eye out. If anyone looks suspicious, we'll take them in for questioning. I doubt if Delgado will show his face but I also don't believe his men will blend in real well."

"Let's go to bed," Madilyn said unexpectedly.

"Bed? Don't you want to eat something?"

"I want you, Brody," she whispered. "I need to feel safe and there's no place I feel safer than in your arms."

Brody stood and put his hand out to her. She placed her hand in his and followed him to the bedroom. He lifted her into his arms and laid her on the bed. He laid down beside her and kissed the tears from her cheeks.

"I won't let him hurt you," he promised.

She reached for the buttons on his khaki shirt and slipped them open. Brody took the shirt off and tossed it to the floor. His hands went to the bottom of her shirt and lifted it over her head. He pressed his lips to hers as he unclasped her bra. Pulling her up, he removed the bra and tossed it. Then his hand roamed down her stomach to the snap of her jeans and lowered the zipper slowly. Brody's hand snaked inside her panties to her feminine folds. She squirmed under his hand.

Madilyn's hands went to the snap of his jeans. His hard shaft strained against the zipper. She lowered it, wrapped her hand around him, and moved her hand up and down the length of him, making him growl low in his throat. Her hands moved to push his jeans down, when one of them encountered the handcuffs. She raised her gaze to his and grinned.

"Why are you grinning?" he asked.

"So...deputy. How often do you get to use these?" She jingled the handcuffs.

He chuckled. "Not as much as I'd like to. Why? What do you have in mind?"

"Handcuff me," she whispered.

Brody took both of her hands in one of his. He put the handcuffs through the bed spindles and hooked them around her wrists. He grinned at her as he ran his hands over her breasts to her stomach.

"Maybe this wasn't such a good idea," Madilyn moaned.

"Oh, I think it's a wonderful idea." Brody chuckled as he moved down her legs and stripped her of her jeans and panties.

Madilyn pulled at the handcuffs. "I want to touch you."

"You should have thought of that before you suggested this. I have you at my mercy."

Madilyn stared up at him. "You've always had me at your mercy, Brody."

"I'm not taking those off you, so don't try to sweet-talk me."

Madilyn growled up at him and then laughed. "Damn it. You know me too well."

Brody leaned down and kissed her. "I'm going to go over every inch of you."

Madilyn groaned. "Brody..."

"Shhh. Leave me alone."

She let out a gasp when he moved his tongue to her breast and took a nipple deep into his mouth. His hand moved down her stomach and down through her curls. He moved his finger up and down her folds, making her wetter. His finger dipped inside. When she moaned, he inserted another finger as his mouth moved over her stomach and down to her clitoris. Brody sucked and moved his tongue over it. She screamed out his name as she came. Madilyn lay there panting, watching Brody roll on a condom. He sat up and pulled her onto his lap, and thrust into her. She wrapped her legs around his waist as he pumped into her.

Madilyn pulled against the handcuffs. She wanted her hands on him but it was exciting as hell with handcuffs on. She watched as Brody dropped his head back while he started slamming against her harder. She started breathing harder as she felt the orgasm coming over her and cried out his name the same instant he groaned out hers. Brody's head dropped forward as she watched him try to catch his breath. His hard pecs rose and fell with each deep breath.

"Take these off me now, please," Madilyn panted out.

Brody leaned down and captured her lips in a deep, hard kiss then he leaned over and removed the key for the handcuffs from his utility belt. After he took the cuffs off, he lay down beside her and pulled her to him. Madilyn needed this all-consuming feeling of him needing her and loving her. He could always make her feel cherished and safe. She really wanted to feel safe. They fell asleep.

Chapter Nine

Wilson Delgado leaned against the fender of his car. The two men he'd hired stood in front of him. They were both huge men. Well over six foot, with each of them weighing close to three hundred pounds. Muscle. Delgado knew he could trust them. They were the same men who'd killed Abby for him. Not very intelligent but they got the job done.

"I want her taken from him as soon as you can. It's not going to be easy, especially since she's living with him now." He moved toward the door and opened it. "I don't want you to hurt her. That's going to be my pleasure. You just get her for me. I want Morgan to know I have her and will kill her." He smirked.

"Boss? How long are you going to keep her alive?" one of the men asked.

Delgado frowned. "You got somewhere you have to be?"

"No, but this town is boring as hell."

Delgado laughed. "Once you grab her, we're out of here. We'll take her to the same spot Abby was killed. So appropriate, don't you think?" He narrowed his eyes at them. "So, how quickly we get out of this hellhole is entirely up to you. Let me know when you have her." He entered his car and pulled away. Glancing in the rearview mirror, he shook his head as he watched the two men staring after him. The sooner this went down, the better.

Delgado grinned as he thought of how Morgan would freak out when he knew Delgado had his woman. The thought of not killing her right away just came to him. He'd keep her as long as he could, just to torment Morgan. After all, Morgan had been with Abby for a while before Delgado had her killed. He'd take great pride in watching her beg for her life, though. The house he'd rented was secluded and no one would hear her screams. He'd paid for an entire year, although he'd be there less than two months. Once he knew Morgan was going crazy looking for her, she'd be killed. Delgado was going to take great joy in letting Morgan know what he planned on doing. He chuckled as he drove toward the house. It wouldn't be long now. All he had to do was wait for his men to grab her and bring her to him. Brody Morgan was going to suffer for a while. Wilson wasn't going to end it for him quickly. He shook his head. No. He was going to keep her alive until Brody begged him to let her go. Then he'd pull Morgan in and kill her in front of him. Wilson shrugged. Maybe he'd just go ahead and kill Morgan too. That way when Wilson took off for Canada, there would be no loose ends. He'd wouldn't need to look over his shoulder all the time. Because he knew, without a doubt, Morgan would hunt him down. Wilson nodded. It would be better to kill him right after Morgan saw the love of his life die.

* * * *

The next morning, Brody stood in the kitchen drinking coffee when Madilyn strolled in. She moved toward him, stood on her toes, and kissed his chin.

"Good morning." She got a cup down and filled it with the dark brew.

"Morning. Did you sleep well?" Brody kissed her head.

"Once I got to sleep, I did. I tossed and turned a good bit first."

"Yes, I know." Brody set his cup down and took her hands in his. "I'll do everything in my power to keep you safe."

Madilyn's arms went around his waist. "I know."

"I'll follow you to work and check the place out before you go in."

"He can't get into the shop, Brody. The alarm would've gone off."

"I'm still checking it out. Humor me." When she nodded, he put his utility belt on and his weapon into his holster. "I'm going to look around outside before we leave. Lock the door behind me." He walked out the door and listened as she locked it. Moving down the steps of the porch, his gaze swept the yard as he headed toward the barn. Opening the door, the scent of horse, hay, and manure assaulted his nose. He smiled, loving every bit of it. He'd recently purchased two horses from Wyatt Stone. Now, to just add some Angus to all of it would make it complete. Brody withdrew his weapon as he slowly moved down the aisle of the barn. Horses whinnied and shifted around but nothing out of the ordinary. Once he walked through both barns, he headed back to the house. The door opened before he reached it. Madilyn stood in the doorway. He stopped in his tracks. This is what he wanted. Her. At the door, waiting for him every day for the rest of his life. Brody moved up the steps and took her in his arms.

"I love you so much, Maddie. I want to marry you now. Today," he whispered before his lips took hers in a deep kiss.

"I love you, too, but we have to wait a little while. Let's see what happens with the shop first."

Brody sighed. "All right. If you're ready, we can leave now."

She nodded up at him. "Yes. I'll be at the shop alone for a while. I forgot to tell you Katie has an appointment with an attorney this morning."

"I'm staying with you until she gets there, then. I'll let Sam know." Brody called Sam quickly and explained the situation. He hung up and grinned at Madilyn. "He's good with it."

"I'm glad. I'd feel better with you there. I don't think Delgado will do anything with Katie at the shop. Too many customers throughout the day, too."

Brody nodded. "That's what I'm thinking."

"Although, if Sam wants to come over for a while, that'd be fine." Madilyn grinned at him.

Brody growled. "Not funny."

Madilyn laughed. "He's gorgeous. What can I say?" Brody grabbed her and pulled her against him. "I'm teasing you, Brody. You're the only man for me."

"Damn good thing, baby." He chuckled against her neck.

"But Sam is gorgeous...just sayin'." She

squealed when Brody nipped at her neck.

"Let's go." He took her hand and led her outside. He waited while she got into her car then he got into his and they drove toward town.

* * * *

Madilyn kept glancing toward the rearview mirror. Watching Brody following her made her feel safe. Wilson Delgado had an agenda and she was terrified of him accomplishing it. She sighed with relief when she pulled into the parking lot at the shop. Stepping from her car, she stood beside it as she watched Brody park his truck and stroll toward her.

"I'd rather you stay in the car until I get to you, Maddie. I don't want to scare you, but he could be anywhere at any time." Brody shook his head. "Since we don't know what he has planned, I want to be at your side when we're alone."

Madilyn nodded and glanced around quickly. "I hadn't thought of that. I won't do it again."

"It's all right. I should've mentioned it. Come on, let's get inside."

Madilyn unlocked the door then turned the alarm off. She moved behind the counter and waited while Brody moved through the building. He came back toward her and smiled.

"All clear. Do you have a coffee pot here? I could use another cup."

"Sure. I'll make some. I'll be right back." Madilyn kissed his cheek as she headed for the break room. She went about making coffee then poured him a cup. She halted in the doorway as she stared at him. Her heart slammed against her ribs. How did she ever think she'd get over him? He was the love of her life. Her gaze ran over his back to his jeans hugging his butt. The man had one hell of a body. She watched him spin around to face her and blushed when he raised an eyebrow at her.

"Were you just checking out my ass?" Brody grinned.

Madilyn laughed. "Yes." She moved toward him and handed him his coffee.

"At least you're honest, hon." Brody chuckled. "What time do you think Katie will be here?"

"She really shouldn't be too late. The appointment was at nine." Madilyn smiled. "Speak of the devil." She nodded toward the door as Kaitlyn strode through it.

"Hi Katie," Brody said, and then frowned at the look on her face. "Is something wrong?"

Kaitlyn shook her head. "I'm in shock. Kevin had a life insurance policy and I'm the beneficiary."

Madilyn hugged her. "That's great, Katie. Maybe it was his way of making up for treating you badly."

"It's for a million," Kaitlyn whispered.

"As in dollars?" Brody asked in a shocked voice.

"Oh my God! That's fantastic, Katie. You can pay your house off now." Madilyn smiled at her.

"I'm going to sell it. I don't want to live there. I'll get an apartment for now and maybe after the baby's born, I'll buy another home." Kaitlyn smiled at Madilyn. "I'm going to buy the shop, though."

"What?" Madilyn squealed.

Kaitlyn hugged her. "We have jobs and you're going to be manager. We'll hire a couple more people so I'll be able to take time off when the baby's born."

"I'm so happy. Not just for us having jobs but for you Katie. You deserve this. Did you tell Sam yet?" Madilyn hugged her friend.

"I did. He's in shock, I think. I called him as soon as I left the attorney's office."

Brody chuckled. "I'm heading to the office." He quickly kissed Madilyn on the lips and kissed Kaitlyn's cheek.

Madilyn and Kaitlyn started their day. Customers came in all day long but neither of the women could keep the smiles from their faces. Madilyn stood beside Kaitlyn as she called the real estate office to tell them she wanted to buy the shop.

"I'm going to ask Sam if I can have a party at the ranch. I'll invite everyone." Kaitlyn giggled.

"What a great idea, Katie. I can help you plan it. I think it'll be fun." Madilyn laughed.

"It'll be to celebrate my buying the shop and the baby." Kaitlyn laughed again. "I'm so excited."

Madilyn loved seeing her friend happy again. It'd been too long since Kaitlyn was happy. She deserved to be after living with a man like Kevin. Madilyn thought of Brody. The one time he'd hurt her had been her fault, not his. She should've supported him in his decision to become a Marshal and gone with him. They would've had the past five years together and probably had a couple of children by now. A boy and a girl like they'd always talked about. Madilyn hated herself for blaming Brody when it had been her fault for not going with him. How could he forgive her when she found it hard to forgive herself? He loved her. It was as simple as that. She smiled. What a wonderful man he was. Another customer came in and Madilyn moved forward to wait on her.

* * * *

Brody strolled through the front door of the department and sent a smile over to Betty Lou. She narrowed her eyes at him.

"What are you doing here during the day, Brody?"

Brody halted. "Didn't Sam tell you? I'm on days for a while."

"No, he didn't tell me. I wondered where Rick was." Betty Lou stood and put her hands on her hips. "What's going on?"

"Nothing at all, Betty Lou." Brody quickly moved toward his office. He almost faltered in his steps when she spoke.

"I'm not stupid, Brody Morgan. Something is going on for Sam to change your shift." She huffed. "No one tells me anything," Brody heard her mutter as he closed the door to his office. The woman wasn't lying. She wasn't stupid but Brody also knew Sam wouldn't tell her anything he didn't want half the town knowing. As much as Sam loved Betty Lou, they both knew she was a major gossip in Clifton.

Brody sat at his desk and got to work on some paperwork. An hour later, he heard Betty Lou giving Sam a hard time. Brody chuckled and shook his head. Better Sam than him. He jerked when his door flew open. Sam stood in the doorway.

"I'll never hear the end of this," Sam mumbled as he took a seat in front of Brody's desk.

"She tried to get it out of me. I got back here as quickly as I could."

"You could've called me. I would've come in the back door." Sam glared at him.

Brody laughed. "Betty Lou would have hunted you down. You know it as well as I do."

Sam chuckled. "I do for sure. Did everything go all right getting Madilyn to work?"

"Yes. Katie wasn't too late." Brody grinned as Sam shook his head. "Can you believe he made her beneficiary?"

"No. It's the only decent thing he ever did for Katie. She's on cloud nine. I think it's a great idea for her to buy the shop. She loves the place."

"I was still there when she told Maddie. Both women are happy as can be. Maybe this will keep Maddie's mind off Delgado some."

"Let's hope so." Sam stood. "I'll be in my office. Let's hope we have a slow day and you can get out of here on time. If not, I'll get Madilyn over here to wait. I don't want her alone at any time."

Brody nodded as Sam left his office. Luckily, it turned out to be the slow day they'd hoped for and Brody left at five to head to the shop. He strolled through the doors and smiled at Kaitlyn while she waited on a customer. He watched her move away from the customer and moved toward him.

"Madilyn's in the break room."

Brody

Brody nodded. "I'll go back there then." He headed for the break room and stood in the doorway. "Hey baby." She spun around and dropped the glass she'd been holding. Brody moved quickly. "Step back. I'm sorry, I didn't mean to scare you." He knelt down and started picking up the glass shards. He jerked his head up when he heard her crying. "What is it?"

"I'm so afraid," she whispered.

Brody stood and wrapped his arms around her. "I know. I can't tell you not to be afraid. He's dangerous as hell but if you're afraid, you'll be more alert and I want you alert."

"I wasn't very alert now."

"Only because you feel safe here. Don't let your guard down anywhere. Not even here. Any customer coming through those doors could be someone he sent in here." Brody gazed down into her face. "Do you understand?"

Madilyn nodded up at him. "I won't be so jumpy the next time."

"That's my girl. Now, let me clean this up and we'll go home." They cleaned up the glass and after telling Kaitlyn they'd see her tomorrow, they left.

* * * *

A week later, practically the entire town of Clifton, including tourists, was in the Town Hall for Kaitlyn's party. Her plan to have it at the ranch soon became evident it needed to be in a larger place since so many people planned on attending. Madilyn stood beside her friend at the table with large plates and bowls of food. A line of people moved down the table, getting food and talking away with the person next to them. Betty Lou Harper stopped in front of Madilyn and Kaitlyn.

"It's good to see both you girls smiling." Betty Lou smiled at them.

Kaitlyn laughed. "I'm happy, Betty Lou. For the first time in a long time."

Betty Lou chuckled. "You deserve it honey, and so do you, Madilyn." She leaned forward. "Now, Katie, you just need to get your brother happy."

"Sam's not happy?" Madilyn frowned.

"He needs a woman," Betty Lou whispered.

"I don't need a woman and you're holding up the line, Betty Lou," Sam growled. The people in line laughed.

"You do, Sam Garrett," Betty Lou mumbled as she moved on.

Madilyn grinned at Sam. "She loves you and wants to see you happy, Sam."

"I am happy, damn it."

Madilyn and Kaitlyn laughed along with the people in line. The smile left Madilyn's face when Brody moved up to the table. Their eyes met and held.

"Hi," he said softly.

"Hi yourself, Deputy Morgan." Madilyn smiled at him.

Brody nodded. "You make sure you call me that when I'm in uniform, ma'am. Otherwise, I may have to handcuff you."

Madilyn could feel the heat in her cheeks as she gazed at him. The memories came rushing back of her handcuffed to the bed. Her eyes instinctively went to the fly of his jeans and back to his face.

"I'll keep it in mind...Deputy," Madilyn said softly. She jerked when Kaitlyn elbowed her. She turned her gaze to her friend, who nodded to the line of people. Madilyn looked at them to see them all staring at her and Brody. She bit her lip to keep from laughing at the look on their faces. "You're holding up the line, Deputy. Please move along."

Brody chuckled as he put food on his plate and moved on. Madilyn blew out a breath. She heard Kaitlyn chuckle beside her.

"I love watching people in love." Kaitlyn sighed. "I want to be in love like that."

"I can't believe you'd say that, Katie, after the relationship you just went through."

"Madilyn, you went through a tough time, too. Brody left and you were alone but look at you now. You're both so in love, like the years faded away. I want that all-consuming love in my life too. I thought I had it when I first married Kevin but I didn't. I want it. I want to find *the* one." Kaitlyn shook her head. "I want a man in love with me. To worship me." She gazed around the room. "Like Jake and Becca. Emma and Gabe. They have it."

Madilyn's gaze followed Kaitlyn's to where the Stone family stood. Jake and Becca were laughing together. Gabe was no doubt teasing Emma about something since her cheeks were red. Gabe held their little girl, Sophie, who he adored. All of them were so much in love. Her eyes roamed over the room until she found

Brody. He stood next to Sam, his eyes constantly searching the room. When they met hers, he smiled at her. Madilyn smiled. She loved him so much. Nothing was going to tear them apart again. She'd follow him to the ends of the earth if need be. Sighing, she brought her attention back to the people in line and smiled up at the man in front of her. She didn't recognize him but with all the tourists in town, it was nothing new for some of them to wander into the Town Hall while something was going on. He grinned at her. Madilyn shivered. He didn't seem to fit in with the other tourists. Most of the tourists were families. This man looked like he belonged anywhere but Clifton, Montana. He could've stepped from a movie involving the mob.

"What's your name, little lady?" he asked her.

Madilyn smiled up at him. "What can I get you?"

He grinned at her change of subject. "Everything looks good. Including you."

The smile left her face. "You're holding up the line."

The man chuckled. "Feisty, too. I like that." He leaned toward her. "You're going to need to be." Then he spun on his heel and disappeared through the crowd. Madilyn moved quickly toward Brody and Sam.

"There's a man you need to find. He sort of threatened me and then left. I can't see him now." Madilyn scanned the crowd.

"What did he look like?" Brody was on instant alert.

"Big. He was so out of place, in a black suit.

It's why he stood out to me. Then he said I was feisty and I was going to need to be." She grasped Brody's arm. "He looked like he belonged to the mob."

Brody and Sam both set their plates down and moved through the crowd toward the doors. They disappeared outside. Madilyn jerked when Kaitlyn touched her arm.

"Are you all right? You're as white as a sheet."

Madilyn nodded. "I had to let Brody know about the man in line." She'd told Kaitlyn about Delgado and she knew to be on the lookout for any strangers who didn't fit in with the tourists. "He stuck out like a sore thumb. Brody and Sam went outside to look for him but I'd bet money they won't find him. He disappeared through the crowd and out the door before I even told them."

"I think you're right. They just came back in." Kaitlyn nodded toward the door.

Brody and Sam came toward them. Brody shook his head. "We couldn't find him. He must've taken off before we got outside." Brody took her hands in his. "He planned this. He knew what he was going to say to you and how to get out fast. The crowd helped him out."

Madilyn needed to sit down. "I feel lightheaded," she whispered. Brody led her through the doors leading to the kitchen, Sam and Kaitlyn on their heels. Brody pulled a chair out and pushed her down onto it.

"Take deep breaths," Kaitlyn told her.

Madilyn sucked in deep breaths. She glanced up at Brody. "He knew who I was, didn't he?"

"Yes," Brody told her.

"Oh dear God. He knows me."

Brody crouched down in front of her. "I'll keep you safe. He can't get to you. As long as you're never alone, he can't get to you."

"I want to go home." She glanced up at Kaitlyn. "I'm sorry to leave your party early, Katie..."

"Nonsense. Go home, Madilyn. I'd feel better if you did."

"Come on, Maddie. Let's go home." Brody glanced at Sam. "Is it all right if we leave?"

"Yes. Take her home. I'll see you tomorrow. I'll keep an eye out here but I'm sure he's gone for now." He narrowed his eyes. "Do not let your guard down. The son of a bitch is going to do all he can to get to her."

Madilyn stood and let Brody lead her out and to the cars. "Do you think you can drive or do you want to go with me?"

"I can drive," she assured him.

Brody softly kissed her lips. "I'll be right behind you."

Madilyn watched him stride to his truck. Once he was in it, she started her car and pulled out with Brody behind her. She quickly blinked tears away. Seeing the man, knowing he was one of Delgado's men, put it all into perspective. Delgado was letting her know he meant what he'd said. He planned to get to her and kill her to make Brody suffer. She had to pull off the road. Brody was at her window in less than a minute. He pulled her door open and squatted down.

"Oh, baby. I'm so sorry. Come here." He held his arms out to her.

Madilyn leaned toward him and wrapped her arms around his neck. "It's all real now."

"I know and I'm sorry this is happening." He kissed her forehead. "Let it out."

Madilyn choked back a sob and then let go. She sobbed on his shoulder. The terror she felt was unreal. "I've never been so scared in my life."

"I know, baby. I know." Brody sighed. "I'll keep you safe. I promise."

Madilyn couldn't stop crying. She'd never been as terrified of anything as she was of this. Wilson Delgado, who wanted to kill her and she knew he'd stop at nothing to achieve his goal. He hated Brody and making him suffer was all he wanted. She pulled back from Brody and placed her palm on his cheek.

"I don't want him to hurt you either," she whispered.

"As much as I hate saying this, I have to. He isn't worried about killing me. Getting to you will be his way of hurting me. He won't kill me. He knows taking you from me will be as if he put a gun to my head and pulled the trigger."

Madilyn stared at him as tears rolled down her cheeks. "We have to be careful of everything. Everywhere we go, we have to be alert. As Sam said, we can't let our guard down." She leaned forward and kissed him. "I love you so much, Brody."

"I love you too, Maddie. I always have and I always will." He stood. "Now let's go home."

Madilyn nodded and started her car. She watched Brody go back to his truck and get in. Once she heard the engine start, she pulled out and sighed with relief when he pulled out behind her. She felt immensely better when she pulled into the driveway and up to the back of the house.

Chapter Ten

Brody walked toward her car and stood beside it as she opened the door. She was so pale it worried him. He had to get her inside and protect her. He'd die before he let Delgado get to her. Living without her wasn't going to happen. For five years, he'd lived without her and thought of her every day, now with her back in his life, he'd be damned if anyone was going to take her away from him.

He smiled at her as she clutched his arm. Brody's eyes scanned the yard then came back to her. "I want you to get back in your car and lock the door. I want to check the house. Do not get out of the car. Blow the horn if you see anything out of place or if someone comes up to the car. If I'm not back in fifteen minutes, leave and call Sam. Don't argue with me, Maddie. Do as I say."

Madilyn's gaze swiftly roamed the yard. "Did you see something?" she asked.

"No but I want to check the house before we both go in. Please, just listen to me."

She nodded and got into the car and locked the door. Brody gave a terse nod and moved toward the house. Taking his weapon from his holster, he entered the house. It was just a feeling he had. He wasn't sure what it was yet but there was no way Madilyn was entering the house until he checked it out. With his gun held in front of him, he slowly walked through the kitchen and into the living room. Call it a cop's intuition but he had a feeling someone had been there. He moved down the hallway and into each bedroom, opening closet doors. Nothing was amiss. The feeling of someone being there intensified when he entered his bedroom. He quickly opened the closet doors, encountering no one.

Brody sighed and put his gun in his holster. No one was there now but he knew someone had been. He quickly walked to the front door and checked the lock, but it didn't look as if it'd been tampered with. The back door was good, too. He signaled for Madilyn to come in and watched as she practically ran to him, throwing herself into his arms.

"I've got you. I've got you." He told her over and over. Her body shook as she wrapped her arms around his waist. Brody kissed the top of her head. "Come on. Let's go into the living room so you can rest. He shook you to the core. You need to relax."

"Don't leave me," she pleaded.

"Never, darlin'. I'll never leave you again." Brody led her to the living room and helped her take a seat on the couch. "Why don't you lie down?"

"Will you stay here?"

"Yes, I'll just sit over there and watch television. I won't go anywhere. I promise."

Madilyn lay down and closed her eyes while he took a seat in the chair and picked up the remote. He still couldn't shake the feeling someone had been in the house.

* * * *

Two weeks passed with nothing happening. No phone calls from Delgado and no sight of the man from the party. It was as if they'd disappeared. Madilyn wasn't as jumpy as she was weeks ago. She'd even suggested to Brody that Delgado had given up and moved on.

"He probably got tired of waiting for us to be alone somewhere," she said to him.

Brody shook his head. "You don't know him like I do. He won't give up. Something probably came up and he had to leave for a while. He'll show up."

"You don't know—"

"I *do* know, Madilyn." Brody wrapped his fingers around her biceps. "I'm sorry but I know him. He's evil and once he gets an idea in his head, he won't let go. He's ruthless. Please don't think he's gone or won't come back if he is. I can't have you thinking you're safe until we get him on something and lock him away. Tell me you won't do anything foolish."

Madilyn agreed with him but now since nothing had happened at all, she was convinced Delgado was gone and wouldn't return. He'd seen he couldn't get to her so he left. She continued to tell herself this for days. People came into the shop and wandered around while Madilyn stood at the counter. Kaitlyn was in the office working on shipments. When Sam entered the shop, Madilyn felt the blood drain from her face. She was always afraid Sam was there to tell her Brody was injured or worse. Anytime she saw Sam enter the shop, she was so afraid he was there to give her bad news.

"Madilyn..." Sam stopped at the counter and reached into his pocket. "Is this the man who spoke to you at the party?" He handed her a sheet of paper with a man's picture on it.

She gasped when she saw it. "Yes, that's him. Where did you get this?"

"Mark pulled him over for drunk driving last night. As soon as I saw him this morning, I thought he fit the description you gave." Sam folded the paper and stuck it in his pocket. "I did some background checking on him and he's a known associate of Delgado. There's a warrant on him so I can keep him until Butte sends someone to get him. I just wanted to see if it was the man who spoke to you."

Madilyn grinned up at him. "I'm so glad he's in jail. Does Brody know?"

"Yes. He wanted to tell you but he's out on a traffic accident." Sam smiled at her. "You two can celebrate later." He chuckled when Madilyn's cheeks turned pink. "Where's Katie?"

"In the office working up orders. I've never seen her so happy, Sam. She loves owning the shop. The new sign will be up tomorrow." Madilyn grinned. Kaitlyn had changed the name to Katie's Florist and Greenhouse.

Sam shook his head and grinned. "She's very happy. Did she rope you into helping her move this weekend too?"

Madilyn nodded. "Of course and had me ask Brody too." She laughed. "I don't mind helping. I'm thrilled to death for her."

"Me too. Well, I'd better get back to the office

before Betty Lou sends out the National Guard."

Madilyn burst out laughing. "She would, too. I'll tell Katie you stopped by and thanks for showing me the picture, Sam. Have a great day. Mine just got better."

"Doesn't mean to drop your guard. Until we have Delgado, be on your toes."

Madilyn nodded. "Yes, sir."

"Smart ass," Sam muttered as he strolled away.

Madilyn chuckled as she watched him go out the door. Two women coming in stopped to stare at him. They watched him saunter away before coming inside. Madilyn smiled at them.

"Can I help you ladies with something in particular?"

"I'll take one of those," one woman said, pointing toward Sam.

Madilyn burst out laughing. "I can't help you with that but anything in here, I can."

The women sighed and laughed. Kaitlyn came from the back and stood beside Madilyn.

"These women were interested in your brother," Madilyn teased.

Kaitlyn snorted and gazed at the women. "I doubt if Sam will ever settle down."

"Oh, honey, I don't want to marry him," the woman said.

Kaitlyn and Madilyn laughed. The women headed for the greenhouse. "What was Sam doing here? Is everything all right?" Madilyn explained why Sam had stopped by. Kaitlyn grinned at her. "That's great. One bad man down and one to go. I think Sam and Brody will get

Delgado before too much longer. Then we can all go back to normal. Whatever that is."

Madilyn nodded and headed toward the greenhouse to see if anyone needed help. She couldn't keep the smile from her face as she thought about the man being in jail and not getting out anytime soon. The state of Wyoming would send someone to pick him up from Butte and fly him back. She wondered what the warrant was for but hoped it kept him in jail for quite a while. The thought of him getting out and coming back to Clifton was something Madilyn refused to think about. All that needed done now was for Delgado to be caught for killing his wife. She shivered although the heat in the greenhouse was stifling.

Most of the people were just walking around. It was too hot to be out there for a long time. Madilyn moved back into the air-conditioned foyer. Kaitlyn stood at the counter waiting on a customer. She raised an eyebrow at Madilyn.

"It's so hot out there. I just needed a break."

"No problem. I wasn't reprimanding you, I was just wondering if you were all right."

Madilyn laughed. "You are the boss, though."

"Pffft. Please, we've been together for five years, we aren't employer employee, we're friends who work together." Kaitlyn smiled at her then smiled at the customer. "I'm sorry. Let's get you a beautiful bouquet."

Madilyn headed back toward the break room to get some water. It was unbearably hot today but she felt sick earlier in the morning so it couldn't really be the heat. She lifted the bottle to her lips and froze. *Oh no!* Was it possible? Pregnant? She ran her hand over her flat stomach and then headed for the office to look at the calendar. When was her last period? Madilyn sat at the desk and spun the chair around to face the calendar behind the desk. She counted the days since her last period. She wasn't due for another week.

She blew out a relieved breath. It was just the heat. She wanted a baby with Brody but not yet. They just found each other again and she wanted to wait a while before having a baby. She jumped when Kaitlyn cleared her throat from the doorway. Madilyn glanced up to her.

"Are you all right? I know I just asked you a few minutes ago, but I want to make sure."

"I'm fine Katie. It's just the heat." Madilyn sighed. "I thought for a moment I could be pregnant but I'm pretty sure I'm not."

Kaitlyn tilted her head. "Are you sure?"

"I'm not due until next week, so I'll know for sure. I felt sick this morning but never thought anything of it until the heat was making me feel sick. Thing is, in the five years I've worked here, the heat's never made me sick before and it's been hotter than this."

"I think you need to pick up a pregnancy test to make sure," Kaitlyn said softly.

"Oh, I can't. If I go in the pharmacy and pick one up, it'll be all over town I'm pregnant." Madilyn shook her head. "Brody would hear about it before I'd even have a chance to take the test. Another week isn't going to make a difference."

Kaitlyn sighed. "I suppose you're right."

Madilyn nodded. "Katie, you know how this town is. Do you remember when Olivia went into the pharmacy to get a test for Emma? The entire town had Olivia pregnant by at least five guys, even though she's never been with any of them."

"Yes. Poor Liv. But I hear where you're coming from. The gossip in this town is amazing. Though sometimes it isn't gossip, it's the truth. I wish I would've listened. I never would've married Kevin and put myself through the pain."

Madilyn put her arm around her. "But you also wouldn't have this shop now. So, it turned out just fine for you and you're going to have a beautiful baby."

Kaitlyn beamed. "I am. But you know what? I'd still have the baby even without the shop. The shop is a bonus. It still amazes me Kevin had me as beneficiary. We took the policies out right after we married but I thought he'd change it to his slut."

Madilyn burst out laughing. "I can't believe you said that."

Kaitlyn laughed. "Why not? It's what she was." She sobered. "I'm sorry I shouldn't speak ill of the dead but I don't like cheaters."

"I'm with you there." Madilyn headed toward the door. "I'm going to run over to the apartment and get some more clothes.

"No. Madilyn, you're not supposed to go anywhere alone."

"The man's in jail, Katie, and I don't believe Delgado's still around and even if he is, he won't grab me. He has other people doing his dirty work. It's not far and I'll be right back. I promise." Madilyn hugged her then left.

She drove her car to the complex since the heat was so bad. She parked and ran up the stairs to her apartment. As she unlocked her door and pushed it open, someone put a cloth over her mouth. She struggled as she felt herself losing consciousness then everything went black.

* * * *

Brody left the Sheriff's Department at lunchtime and headed for his ranch. He entered his home and laid his Smith and Wesson 9mm on the counter. He turned toward the refrigerator to make a sandwich when he froze in his tracks. A red rose lay on the table. That was Delgado's M.O., his method of operation. He'd sent Brody a red rose to remind him of Abby once a month on the anniversary of her death. It was her favorite flower. Brody told Holt about it but that was another dead end. It couldn't be proven it was from Delgado. *Son of a bitch!* What did it mean this time? He slowly moved toward it but didn't touch it. He started to shake. It was a message and Brody prayed it didn't mean what he thought it did.

Reaching for his cell phone, he dialed Madilyn's number and got her voicemail. He called the shop but Kaitlyn told him Madilyn left two hours ago since she wanted to pack more clothes. Brody swore. What did she think she was doing, going to her apartment alone? Brody picked up his weapon and ran outside to his truck. He drove like a lunatic to get to Madilyn's apartment. He ran up the steps and pounded on her door. There was no answer. He used the key she'd given him and entered her apartment. It was eerily quiet.

"Madilyn," he shouted as he went from room to room. He entered her bedroom and sat on the bed. Brody knew Delgado had her. Brody reached into his pocket for his cell phone when he noticed a piece of paper on the nightstand beside the bed. He leaned over and read it.

> *How does it feel to lose the woman you love?*

Brody stared at the note until his eyes blurred. He called Sam.

"Delgado has Maddie," he said when Sam answered.

"How do you know?"

While Sam listened, Brody explained about the red rose and the note he found.

"Don't touch anything. I'm on my way," Sam told him.

Brody hung up but he knew there would be no evidence Delgado had been there. He was too good at getting in and out no matter what the situation. Whether it be taking something from someone or murder, he knew how to cover his tracks. He was too smart and that scared Brody more than anything did.

A few minutes later, Sam arrived and dusted for fingerprints.

"You won't find any. He's good," Brody told Sam.

Sam glanced at him. "I still have to do it." Sam straightened and narrowed his eyes at Brody.

"Why didn't you tell me every damn detail, including the rose, which you failed to mention?"

"I'd forgotten about it until I saw it. You might want to dust for prints at my place too."

"Is the rose still there?"

Brody nodded. "I didn't touch it. As soon as I saw it, I called Maddie. When she didn't answer, I called Katie then came here when Katie told me Maddie had left two hours ago to pick up clothes. She wasn't supposed to leave the shop without me." He paced. "Christ, Sam. That bastard will kill her just to torment me."

"We'll find her. He'll get in touch with you."

"I don't think so. I think he'll just kill her." Brody ran his fingers through his hair. "I have to find her. I can't lose her again."

Sam nodded. "I'm sure he'll call to tell you he has her if only to play with you. We'll put a tap on your phone but if he's as smart as you say he is, he won't stay on there long enough to let us home in on him. But if he uses a cell phone to call you, we can narrow his location down by the tower it pings off."

"I just hope he calls," Brody muttered.

Sam moved around to dust for fingerprints while Brody paced. Once Sam finished, Brody drove to the ranch with Sam following him. They went inside the house and Sam took pictures of the rose lying on the table. Then he began dusting for fingerprints. He shook his head when he finished.

"I don't think we're going to get anything. There's nothing on the rose stem, or petals, and the note is clean, too. You're right, he's smart."

"He'll kill her, Sam, just to hurt me. He won't do anything to me. He told Maddie about this being payback. Although I didn't kill Abby, he blames me that she's dead."

"We'll do what we can to find her." Sam sighed. "Too much shit going on in this little town lately."

"I know. Maddie told me about Jake and Becca then Gabe and Emma. What happened to the sleepy little town where nothing ever happened?"

Sam shook his head. "I wish I knew. The only trouble back when we were younger was us."

Brody smiled. "The bunch of us sure raised hell." He sobered. "I have to find her, Sam."

"I should notify MEPA, missing and endangered person advisory."

"I'd rather not notify anyone yet. Let's see if he calls me first. If you notify MEPA, the media gets involved. He'll kill her for sure," Brody told him.

Sam shook his head. "You want me to break protocol on this? Do you realize how much trouble I could get into? We'd both lose our jobs."

"I know and I'm sorry to ask you to do this but anyone else involved guarantees her death," Brody pleaded.

Sam blew out a breath and nodded. "All right, but if we can't find her in forty-eight hours, I'm calling it in."

"I'll go along with that."

Sam glared at him. "You sure as hell don't have a choice, Brody. We will do this my way or not at all."

Brody gave him a terse nod then went to the

living room to sit and wait. The waiting was going to kill him. He wanted to be out there, looking for her. Saving her. He sat forward and clasped his hands together. Praying seemed to be the only option right now. Brody had never been much for praying but he needed to pray now, for her safety and her return to him. His jaw clenched as he thought of what Delgado would do to her.

* * * *

Madilyn slowly woke up and immediately knew she sat tied to a chair. The man stood across the room from her, smiling. She narrowed her eyes at him. "Who are you?"

"You know exactly who I am, Miz Young. I'm sure your lover told you all about him and my wife having an affair."

"My lover?" Madilyn frowned. She wouldn't give this man anything.

He snorted. "Come on, Miz Young. You know I'm not stupid. Far from it. I've been watching you both for a long time. Way before I even called you." He moved toward her. "You do know he was fucking my wife?"

"I have no idea what you're talking about."

Delgado burst out laughing. "You can tell me that all you want, but I know better."

Comprehension dawned. "You're the guy who came to my apartment looking for Caroline, only there wasn't a Caroline, was there?"

"Give the woman a prize. I saw Morgan leave your place, and I wanted to see what you looked like so we could have this nice little chat."

Madilyn stared at him. He was an attractive man in an expensive suit. It was all a façade. "We don't have anything to talk about."

"Oh but we do, Miz Young. I want Morgan to know I'm going to kill you, and you're going to call him for me."

Madilyn shook her head. "No. I won't do it. Brody didn't know she was married."

Delgado laughed. "So, he did tell you. Is that what he told you?" He strode to her and put his face close to hers. "You don't look stupid to me, but yet you believed his lies. He knew. Trust me."

"I trust you about as far as I can throw you. I trust Brody. He'd never lie to me."

"You're a fool. Tell me how a man sees a woman for six months but knows nothing about her. He was a U S Marshal, I'm sure he looked into her background."

Madilyn shook her head. "If Brody told me he didn't know then he didn't know. I won't call him so you can get him here to kill him."

Delgado shook his head. "You won't be here to see me kill him. You'll be dead. I plan on killing you in front of him so he'll suffer because he loves you, just as I suffered when my wife was killed."

"Brody didn't kill your wife. You did," Madilyn screamed at him.

"It was *because* of Morgan she was killed. Same thing in my book. If he hadn't screwed around with her, she'd still be alive. He should've broken it off when he found out she was married."

"He didn't know! Besides, did you ever stop to think she wasn't happy with you? That's why she screwed around." Madilyn knew by the muscle twitching in his cheek, she'd overstepped her bounds. He straightened up and moved away from her.

"I should kill you right now for saying that."

"Then do it," she shouted.

"You're going to call him first, and then while he listens, I'll do it."

"Not happening, asshole."

"I have your cell phone. I'll call him myself."

Madilyn blinked tears away. She would not let this bastard scare her. Shaking her head, she glared at him. He blew out a breath and turned from her. How could she get out of this situation? Glancing around the room, she saw they were in a small room with a kitchenette area, a bed, and a door leading to what she assumed was the bathroom. She remembered Becca Stone telling her she'd tried escaping through a bathroom window when a man obsessed with her abducted her. Becca hadn't gotten away, but Jake rescued her.

"I have to use the bathroom," she told him.

"Fine but you will leave the door open." He moved toward her and untied her hands and feet. Madilyn stood and after giving him a dirty look, entered the bathroom. She saw him standing by the doorway.

"I can't go if you're going to watch me." She placed her hands on her hips and narrowed her eyes at him.

"Then you won't go because I'm not moving." He folded his arms and stared at her.

"At least turn your back."

Delgado grumbled and turned around.

Madilyn knew she had to act quickly. She slammed the door shut and locked it and then moved to the window and pushed it open. She could hear him kicking the door and it was starting to break. Madilyn got out the window and dropped to the ground. Without hesitation, she ran through the woods, screaming. She came out on a road and had no idea where she was. Glancing around, she watched as cars whipped past her on the two-lane road. When she spotted a police car, she ran toward it, waving her arms. Madilyn saw the car pull down a side street and she ran toward it as fast as she could. As she ran in front the woods, someone grabbed her, put their hand over her mouth, and pulled her back into the woods. They spun her around and she gazed up into Wilson Delgado's angry face.

"Scream and I'll kill you right here. Do you understand?" he growled. Madilyn blinked back tears of frustration and nodded. He pulled her along behind him and entered the house. He pushed her toward the bed. "Sit down," he shouted and then paced in front of her. "The next time you pull a stunt like that, I will kill you, and I'll make sure I leave your body where Morgan can find it. I don't necessarily have to kill him." He shrugged. "I just wanted to in case he decides to try to find me but I'll get away. I have a lot of connections, I can disappear."

"Brody doesn't care about me," Madilyn told him.

Delgado laughed. "You don't expect me to believe that, do you? I've seen you together. I know you're staying with him." He put his face close to hers. "I am not a stupid man, Miz Young, so don't treat me like one."

Madilyn stared up at him then glanced away. There was no way she could lie to him. He was a very smart man. He'd bided his time and watched her and Brody. Anyone seeing them together would know they were in love. Delgado was no exception. When she sighed, Delgado laughed.

"As long as we understand each other, we'll get along just fine."

"I have no desire to get along with you. I hate you. You're a murderer."

"Me? I've never, personally, killed anyone but you know what? All that's about to change with you. I'm going to take great pleasure in killing you in front of Morgan. But as I said, pull this little stunt of running again, and I won't wait for my men to get him." He pulled her up from the bed and reached into his pocket to remove her cell phone. "I'll just give him a little call before we move on."

Madilyn watched as he scrolled through her phone. A grin came across his lips. He turned the phone in her direction to show her Brody's picture.

"Please don't do this. Kill me but leave Brody alone. You're right, if you kill me, it will hurt him more. Letting him live with only my memory will slowly kill him. He loves me so much."

"And you love him. You wouldn't be pleading for his life if you didn't. You see, I don't care, though. I saw my wife murdered because of

Morgan and I want him to see your life end too. I want him to watch it happen. I had to wait for another man to get here before I could do anything, since the other idiot got himself arrested for drunk driving, but my two men will have Morgan and he'll be allowed to watch from a distance."

"He's too smart to be taken by your men." Madilyn glared up at him.

"He's not as smart as you seem to think. He let you out of his sight, didn't he?"

Madilyn shook her head. "He didn't know I was going to my apartment. I didn't tell him."

Delgado glared at her. "You lied to him. Just like every other woman. You lied." He pushed her down onto the chair.

Madilyn refused to answer him and make him angrier. Delgado obviously had a very low opinion of women since his wife had an affair and lied to him the entire time. If the man was cold enough to have his wife killed, he wouldn't hesitate to kill Madilyn. A sob caught in her throat as she realized her life could soon be over. Dear God. The thought of Delgado having Brody killed was torture. Even if her life was taken away, she wanted Brody to live and go on with is life.

"Please don't kill him," she whispered and hated herself for pleading with this awful man.

"Don't beg me for your man's life. My wife pleaded for hers too. If I didn't listen to her, why would I listen to you?"

"You didn't kill your wife, though. Your men did. You can let this go." A tear rolled down her cheek.

Delgado strode over toward her, wrapped his hand around her bicep, and pulled her up. "No! I can't let it go. Whether you believe me or not, I loved my wife, but she wanted Morgan and he wanted her. Not you. Her. Abby was in love with Morgan and no matter what he told you, he knew she was married." He shook his head. "No. I won't let it go. What goes around comes around. His time is coming to watch you die."

Madilyn stared at him. He truly believed Brody would be involved with a married woman. She knew better. Brody Morgan had morals. He'd never stoop low enough to do it. Madilyn may have had a sliver of a doubt when he'd first told her but she knew in her heart, he'd told the truth. Abby Delgado lied to him for six months and ended up dead because of it.

"Your wife is the one at fault. She lied to you and Brody. She's dead. Please let this go."

"I've told you she's dead because of Morgan. If he'd kept his hands off her, she'd still be alive and with me," his voice rose in his rant. He raised his hand.

Madilyn covered her face as she waited for him to hit her. When he didn't, she looked up at him. He glared at her with his hand still in the air. He shook his head.

"I've never struck a woman in my life, and I'm not about to start now."

Madilyn stared at him and then burst out laughing. She laughed until tears rolled down her cheeks. When she finally composed herself, she saw him staring at her with narrowed eyes.

"That's rich. You won't hit a woman but you'll kill her." Madilyn shook her head. "I'm supposed to be happy you're not going to hit me?"

"Shut up!" Delgado roared. "I'm calling Morgan now." He dialed Brody's number and waited for him to answer.

"Maddie?" Brody's voice came over the speaker.

"Brody! Don't talk to him. Hang up!" Madilyn yelled.

"Hang up and I'll kill her right now," Delgado growled.

"Let her go. It's me you want, Delgado."

"The only thing I want for you, Morgan, is for you to watch her die and that'll happen soon enough. I just wanted you to know I have your woman and she's going to die because you fucked my wife."

"I'm tired of going over and over this with you, Delgado."

"Not as tired as I am of hearing you deny knowing she was married. I don't believe you."

"If she lied to you, what makes you think she didn't lie to me?" Brody asked.

Madilyn watched Delgado's face get red as he got angry at Brody's words. She knew by the look on his face, the thought never occurred to him. She stood and faced him.

"He's right. If your wife didn't care about lying to her husband, why would she care if she lied to her...lover?" She choked on the word. In her mind, she knew Brody had been with other women over the past five years but in her heart, it cut her to the core. Madilyn let out a yell when

Delgado struck her across the face.

* * * *

"God damn you!" Brody jumped up from the chair. It rolled behind him and slammed into the wall. His office door flew open as Sam came rushing in. Brody put his hand up to stop Sam from speaking, as he nodded toward his cell phone on his desk. Sam gave a terse nod.

Masculine laughter came from the phone. "She's fine. A little slap never hurt anyone."

"You son of a bitch. I'll kill you," Brody growled.

"You're not going to get the chance. I'm going to get to you before you even see me coming. Then I'm going to make sure you see me kill your woman. You're going to watch the woman you love die, just like I watched my wife die because of you. This is your fault, Morgan. You just don't want your woman to know you had an affair with a married woman. No matter what you've convinced your woman or friends, you knew Abby was my wife and you fucked her anyway. You knew she was married, didn't you? *Didn't you?"* Delgado shouted.

Brody glanced up at Sam, who nodded slightly. Brody swallowed. "Yes." He heard Madilyn gasp. He closed his eyes tightly, and clenched his fists. "Now, let her go."

Delgado laughed. "Seeing the look on your woman's face is almost enough for me to let her go, but you still have to pay for what you did."

"I just admitted it. You don't have to kill Madilyn. Take me instead." Brody slowly sat down. He watched as Sam reached for a sheet of paper and wrote something down. He slid the paper toward Brody. *Did the call come from Madilyn's phone?* Brody nodded. Sam wrote again. *Who is her carrier?* Brody wrote it on the paper. Sam nodded and left the office. "Come on, Delgado. I told you the truth. Let's meet up, and I'll trade places with Madilyn."

"It doesn't work that way. An eye for an eye and all, you know. In this case, a woman for a woman. You finally admitting the truth to me doesn't let you off the hook. My wife is dead because of you and soon Miz Young will be dead. I'm going to keep her for a few days, though, to make it even sweeter. I'll be in touch." Delgado disconnected the call.

Brody stared at the phone until Sam entered the office again. "I have the records. He's not in Clifton. The signal's coming from the Hartland area."

"Hartland? How the hell are we going to find him there? We don't have jurisdiction there."

"It's time we call in the FBI and MEPA."

"No, not yet. Come on, Sam. Let me make myself available for Delgado's men to pick me up. It might give me the chance to save her. I'll wear a wire...anything. Just let me do this. Please." His gaze met Sam's and he knew the minute Sam gave in.

"Damn it, Brody. I don't like this. It's going against protocol and we could both be fired."

"I have to take the chance. If we're found out, I'll say you didn't know anything about it. I did this on my own."

"Bullshit. If you go down for this, I'll go down

with you. Let's go over how we're going to do this," Sam told him as he took his seat.

Brody nodded. They worked on their plan for hours before leaving for the day.

Chapter Eleven

Brody sat in the living room, staring at the television. Although it was on, he paid no attention to it. He couldn't get his mind off Madilyn and what she was going through. Brody was sure Delgado left Hartland by now. It'd been three days and no word from the madman yet. It was starting to wear on him. His thoughts were driving him crazy. Trying to sleep was the worst time. He'd hug her pillow to his chest as he lay in the bed, her perfume lingering on it. He couldn't imagine what was going through her head. Was Delgado mistreating her? Was he feeding her? *Son of a bitch!* Brody jumped up and paced. When was he going to call? Was he even going to call?

Brody sighed and headed for the shower. Dear God, please let her be all right. He'd already lost her once, he couldn't lose her again. Not until he took his dying breath and he hoped when he did, her face was the last thing he saw before he met his maker. They'd always talked about having children. A boy and a girl. Madilyn had laughed and asked him what happened if they had two of the same? Brody told her they'd just keep trying until they got a different one. He smiled as he remembered the look on her face then she burst out laughing and punched his arm. That was the day his dad almost caught them in the hayloft.

Madilyn had put her hand over her mouth to quiet her laughter. Tears rolled down her cheeks as Brody's dad strolled down the barn aisle calling for them. Brody glared at her but had trouble containing his own laughter. When they walked into the house hand in hand, his mom grinned but turned her back. Brody's dad walked into the kitchen and up to Madilyn. He reached out, pulled a piece of straw from her hair, and winked at her. Brody glanced to his mother to see her shoulders shaking from laughter. Even Brody felt the heat in his face that day.

The hot water glided down his body. His muscles were so tense from worry. He needed her home and safe. He'd kill Delgado with his bare hands if he hurt Madilyn in any way and he didn't care what happened to him after he did. The man was a psychopath. He had to be to have his wife killed for being unfaithful.

Brody groaned when he remembered how Madilyn had gasped when he admitted to knowing Abby was married when he was with her. She'd been shocked to hear him confess to it. Shaking his head, he reached for the towel, dried off and then pulled a clean shirt and jeans on. He knew there was another long, sleepless night in front of him. As he walked into the bedroom, someone hit him on the back of the head. Brody did everything he could to stay conscious. Another blow knocked him out.

* * * *

Madilyn lay on the bed and stared at the ceiling. She had no idea where they were. He wasn't mistreating her but he was still going to kill her. He made sure he told her on a daily basis. She hadn't slept much at all in the past three days. Especially since hearing Brody confess to knowing Abby Delgado was married at the time he was seeing her. Sleeping with her. Brody knew Madilyn frowned on cheating and would never forgive a man cheating on her. To her, both people were at fault. The married one for cheating on their spouse and the one they cheated with for getting involved with a married person. Madilyn felt a tear roll down her temple into her hair. How could he do that and then lie about it? If she got out of this situation, she'd never forgive him. It was over between them and it was killing her. Twice now, she'd lost him. He'd looked her in the eye and told her he didn't know Abby was married and she believed him. She was a fool.

"Get up. We're moving right after I call Morgan. I think I've let him stew enough for the past few days," Delgado told her.

Madilyn sighed and sat up. She wiped the tears away, refusing to let him see her fear. She stared up at him. "What does it matter if I see where you take me? You're going to kill me."

"I'm not taking any chances with you. You've already tried getting away once."

"Yes, and you told me you'd kill me if I tried again. Which makes no sense since you tell me you're going to kill me anyway." She shook her head.

"I don't have to make sense to you. All I have to do is get Morgan in a position to see me kill you."

"Then you'll let him go?"

Delgado laughed. "I really don't think I can. I

know damn well he'll come after me. No matter where I'd go, I'd be looking over my shoulder and I don't want to do that."

"But you said you wanted him to suffer by killing me. You lied the entire time," Madilyn's voice rose.

"I was going to let him live, but I don't want him looking for me."

Madilyn shook her head, confused. "He's not going to suffer at all then. You just want to kill us both."

"He'll suffer when he sees you die. I'm going to let him live for a while, just to watch the pain he's in. Just like the pain I was in when I watched the woman I love die."

"You had her killed!" Madilyn shouted.

Delgado strode over to her and put his face close to hers. "It doesn't matter," he said through clenched teeth. "My wife died because she was fucking your man and he's going to pay for it." He pushed her back onto the bed. "If I wanted to be really horrible, I'd rape you, but I'm not into that."

"Thank God for small favors," she muttered as she glanced at his fly.

"You can say whatever you like. You'll be..." The ringing of his cell phone interrupted him. "What is it?" He listened to the caller then laughed. "Fantastic. What? Of course you can kick his ass, just don't kill him." He hung up and laughed. "It seems my man has Morgan. He's going to teach him a little lesson about fucking with another man's wife, and then you and I are going to take a ride."

* * * *

The water thrown on his face woke him up. He coughed and spit the water out. A burly guy stood in front of him. Brody blinked the water from his eyes and glared up at him.

"Wake up, pretty boy," the man laughed.

"Fuck you."

The man burst out laughing. "I want you to wake up so I can kick your ass."

Brody pulled against the ropes holding his hands. "How about untying me, and we'll see who does the ass kicking."

"I can't do that. I have to take you somewhere when I get a phone call."

Brody grinned. "You're afraid I can kick your ass." He grunted when the man slammed his fist into his jaw. Brody spit blood out. "It's pretty fucking bad you have to have a man tied up so you can beat him up. Untie me you asshole." His head snapped back when he took a shot to the chin.

"Keep talking. All you're doing is pissing me off. I'm not stupid enough to untie you."

"But you are some stupid."

"What the fuck do you mean?" The man fisted his hand in Brody's hair and pulled his head back.

"I mean you're a stupid motherfucker—" A fist to his cheek stopped him. Brody could feel his eye swelling shut.

"I can do this all day. Just keep talking."

Brody tilted his head forward and spit more blood out. He slowly raised his head and glared up at the guy. "You might be able to do it all day with me tied to a chair but you untie me and we'll see just how long you can."

"Shut up." He threw a fist at Brody's face, snapping his head back.

Brody kept his head back trying to catch his breath and figure out how to get out of this. He heard the cell phone ring and listened as the man answered it. He spoke in low tones then hung up.

"Looks like we're going for a ride." He walked toward Brody and cut the ropes binding him to the chair. "Get up." He wrapped his hand around Brody's arm and pulled him up from the chair. Brody put his head down and tackled the man. They both tumbled to the floor. Brody sat up, straddling the man. His fists pounded into the man's face.

"Tell me where we're going," Brody demanded.

"Go to hell." The man's fist connected with Brody's jaw, knocking him onto his back. The man jumped up and ran toward him. Brody was ready for him as he kicked his foot out and caught the man in the groin. He doubled over. Brody got to his feet and punched the man in the kidneys.

"You're going to take me where you're supposed to." Brody took the man's gun from inside his jacket and aimed it at him. "Get up. We're leaving."

"Delgado will kill me."

"I'll kill you if you don't take me or tell me," Brody growled. "I know he wants me to watch him kill Madilyn, so tell me now and I'll let you live."

The man laughed. "You won't kill me. If you do, you'll never find her."

"You're right." Brody nodded. "But that doesn't mean I can't shoot you until you do."

The man's eyes widened. "You can't do that."

"Try me," Brody said quietly. When the man didn't say anything, Brody pointed the gun at his leg. "Now."

"All right. All right. I'm supposed to meet him at an abandoned warehouse outside of town."

Brody knew the warehouse he was talking about. It had been a sawmill, at one time. He nodded. "Come on. We're going to the sawmill, and you're going to let Delgado think you've got me. I will have this gun pointed at your head at all times and once I call the sheriff, he'll have a rifle on you." Brody grinned. "Trust me, the sheriff won't hesitate to take you out. Now, let's go."

Brody got into the back of the car and kept the gun on the man as he drove toward the warehouse. Brody called Sam to let him know what was going on. Sam told him he was on his way. When they pulled up to the warehouse, the man got out and opened the back door. Brody stepped out.

"Remember what I said. I'll kill you in a heartbeat." Brody walked in front of him. "Make any sudden move or try to let Delgado know and I'll turn around and shoot you. Understand?"

"Yes," the man muttered.

They slowly entered the warehouse. Brody stopped to let his eyes adjust and he almost ran forward when he saw Madilyn on her knees in front of Delgado. He stood behind her with a gun pointed at the back of her head and a grin on his face as he saw Brody.

"The time has finally arrived for my revenge." Delgado laughed.

Madilyn's hands were bound behind her back and tape over her mouth. Tears streaked down her cheeks. Brody wanted to rush toward her and take her in his arms. He stared at her. When her eyes met his, she glared at him. What the hell? Then it came to him. She believed the lie he'd told Delgado.

"It was a lie, Maddie," he told her and watched as her eyes widened. Then she closed them tightly as tears squeezed through them.

"What are you talking about, Morgan?" Delgado demanded.

"I never knew Abby was married. It was a lie I told you so you wouldn't kill her before you and I met up. Abby lied to both of us, Delgado. She hid it well. Think about it. She hid things from you too. She was seeing me for six months. How many months did she lie to you before you found out?"

"Shut up," Delgado yelled.

"You can't accept the fact your wife lied to you, cheated on you, and God knows what else behind your back. You're blaming me for her death when I had nothing to do with it. Why do you think she cheated? You made her miserable, you piece of shit. She was happy with me and that just tears you up. Someone else made your wife happy. Not you."

"Shut up!" Delgado's face was red with anger.

Brody tried to get Madilyn's attention but she wouldn't look at him. He wanted to let her know to be ready to move.

"The truth hurts, doesn't it, Delgado? Your wife was in love with me. Did you know she told me she'd leave you to run away with me?" Madilyn looked over at him. Brody's eyes caught hers. "She wanted to go wherever I wanted her to. Abby was willing to run when I told her." He almost sighed with relief at the slight nod of her head.

"You filled her head with lies. Do you know how much she pleaded for her life? She begged. She swore you were only friends."

"What does that tell you? She lied up until the end. To you and me both. Why don't you just let us go and move on?"

"I'm going to kill you both. It will make me feel so much better." Delgado shoved the gun against Madilyn's head.

Brody glanced around then back to Delgado. "You'll go to prison or die here."

Delgado laughed. "I'm not going to do either. After I kill your woman, Gus will kill you while I'm heading for Canada."

"Now you see, that's where you're wrong." Brody glanced over his shoulder. "Isn't that right, Gus?"

Brody watched Delgado's eyes go to the man behind Brody then back to him. "I pay him enough not to do anything stupid. You don't have enough money in the world to get him to betray me."

"Maybe not, but I do have his gun. Maddie,

run!" Brody shouted as he shot at Delgado. He felt Gus's hand grab onto his shoulder as Delgado fired back. Blood splattered his face as the bullet hit Gus between the eyes. Brody spun around and fired at Delgado again.

"Maddie! Get out of here." He fired his gun to where Delgado was hiding. "Now!" He watched her run out the door and then ducked when Delgado shot at him. "Give it up, Delgado. You're surrounded."

"Fuck you! I'll die first."

"I don't have a problem with that," Brody mumbled. He saw Delgado stand and aim his weapon toward him when his body jerked and he fell to the floor. Brody slowly made his way toward him and stared down at Delgado lying in a puddle of blood flowing from his shoulder. "Looks like it's going to be prison."

Delgado moaned and stared up at him. "Why didn't you just kill me?"

"I would have if I'd been the one to shoot you. I believe it was the sheriff who shot you." Brody shook his head. "He knew I'd kill you if I had the chance." Brody stared down at him. "Damn you, Sam." Brody called him. "Get an ambulance and the coroner. You got Delgado in the shoulder." Brody laughed as he listened to Sam on the phone. "Of course I'm disappointed you only wounded him." Brody glanced down at Delgado. "If he tries to run I'll shoot to kill." He turned toward the door when it opened. Madilyn came running toward him. He caught her in his arms and slowly removed the tape from her mouth.

"I'm so sorry," she cried.

"For what?" He asked as he untied her hands.

"Letting him get me."

"Oh yeah. You and I are going to have a talk about that." Brody pressed his lips to hers. "I could've lost you." He tried to deepen the kiss as her arms moved around his neck but it hurt too much.

"I'm also sorry I doubted you. When I heard you tell him you lied about knowing she was married, I should've realized it was a trick. I'm so sorry. I believe you."

When the door opened, Brody moved her behind him, and then he sighed when he saw Sam enter. "Please tell me you missed when you shot Delgado."

Sam huffed. "I don't miss. I hit him exactly where I aimed."

"Damn it," Brody muttered. "I suppose him sitting in prison will have to do."

Sam nodded and glanced at Madilyn. "Are you all right? Did they hurt you in any way?"

"I'm fine, Sam. I just want to go home."

"You'll need to come to the department to make a statement. It can wait until tomorrow. You need some rest. I'm sure you haven't had much lately."

"Thank you, Sam. I am tired." Madilyn gazed at Brody. "You look terrible."

"He had me tied to a chair and hit me. I'll be fine." Brody winced when Madilyn put her fingers to his busted lip and then his swollen eye.

"I know," she whispered.

The paramedics came through the door with a stretcher and headed toward Delgado. He shouted out in pain as they lifted him. Brody grinned. "Damn shame you're in such pain, Delgado."

"I'll get out and kill you, Morgan," Delgado shouted.

"Threatening an officer of the law, Delgado?" Sam stepped forward. "There's some added charges." He glanced at the paramedics. "Get him out of here. Deputy Mark Shaw will follow you and stay posted outside the room."

"Do you think he'll get out of going to prison?" Madilyn asked.

"Not a chance in hell, baby. He's going away for a long time. We're free of him." Brody hugged her to him. "Let's go home."

"Do you need to go to the hospital, Brody?"

"No, I'm fine. We're going home, Maddie. I want to sleep for about a week."

She laughed. "Me too." Madilyn wrapped her arm around his waist as he put his arm around her shoulder. They told Sam goodbye and headed out the door to go home.

When Brody pulled up to the back door, they both sat in the car not moving. He reached his hand over to her. "Are you really all right, Maddie?"

She nodded. "I am now. I'm so glad to be home and with you."

"Come here." Brody whispered. She slid across the seat and Brody pulled her across his lap. He laid his forehead against hers. "We're fine now. He'll never hurt us again."

Madilyn's fingers ran lightly over his busted lip. "I'm so sorry they did this to you."

He tried to smile but it hurt too much. "It'll heal. All of it will heal and we're going to move on with our lives. I love you, baby. We're going to get married and raise our babies here."

"Yes. I want that so much." A tear rolled down her cheek. Brody caught it with his finger. "I wish Sam would've killed him, though."

"Sam goes by the book. He wouldn't be able to live with himself if he'd killed Delgado for the hell of it. Although, I'm sure Sam wanted to."

"I didn't know Sam was so good with a rifle. I've never heard of him shooting. I remember he had Wyatt Stone shoot the man in the church tower at Becca and Jake's reception."

"Sam told me about it. He had to try to talk the guy down. He knew Wyatt could take the shot and not kill him." Brody shook his head. "I'd hate to choose between the two of them who's better. Let's go inside and get some rest. A shower sounds good right about now."

She nodded and slid across the seat. They went inside and headed for the bathroom. Brody took her hands in his and gazed into her eyes. "I want you so much but I'm exhausted."

Madilyn smiled up at him. "We have all the time in the world now, deputy. Let's shower and take a nap. Maybe when we wake up..." She shrugged.

Brody chuckled. "You got a deal." They took a shower and then slept.

* * * *

Two hours later, Madilyn woke up and glanced over to Brody to see he was still sleeping. Slowly crawling from the bed, she made her way across the room when her gaze fell on his utility belt laying across the chair. Quickly glancing at him again, she reached for the handcuffs on the belt and removed them. She tiptoed back to the bed and crawled up his body softly so as not to disturb him. Madilyn slowly raised his arms to above his head and handcuffed him to the headboard. Sitting up to straddle him, she ran her fingernails down his chest. He jerked awake.

"Maddie? What are you doing?" he asked in a sleepy voice.

"I'm putting you under house arrest, Deputy Morgan." She laughed softly.

"What..." He tried to move his hands but glanced above his head to see them handcuffed. He narrowed his eyes at her. "Just what do you think you're doing, Madilyn?"

Madilyn grinned down at him. "Payback's a bitch, Brody." She laughed when he pulled at the handcuffs.

"Un-cuff me," he growled.

"No." She leaned down and kissed him. "I won't hurt you. I'll be gentle," she whispered against his lips.

"Madilyn..." His plea ended on a groan when she ran her tongue down his neck to his chest. "I want to touch you."

Madilyn sat up. "It seems I wanted the same thing when you had me in this, uh...predicament, and you didn't listen. Just relax, baby. I'll take care of you." She kissed her way down his chest to his nipples and ran her tongue over them. He squirmed.

"Damn it. Take these off me," he groaned.

She laughed. "No. I've got you where I want you, Brody Morgan."

"You've always had me where you wanted me," Brody said.

"Telling me things like that will not grant your freedom. I intend to have my way with you." She smiled against his stomach when he growled low in his throat. Madilyn felt his erection under the sheet as she straddled him. She pulled the sheet back, wrapped her hand around him, and kissed the head, making him hiss out a breath. Her mouth moved down the length of him and back up, taking him deep into her mouth. She sucked on him and ran her tongue around the head. His hips rose up off the bed. His groans encouraged her.

* * * *

Brody's hands jerked against the handcuffs. *Damn it!* She was killing him. When her tongue ran down the length to his balls, he growled. He refused to beg. Hell, he needed to beg.

"Maddie, baby, please. I can't take this much long..." He broke off when she put her mouth over him again and suckled, taking him deep into her mouth. He started panting. He was getting too close. "I want to be inside you."

She chuckled softly. "You are inside me."

"You're such a fucking smart ass," he moaned. She sat up and stared down at him. His eyes met hers. "Come on, take these off. Let me touch you."

She stretched out over him, reaching for the handcuffs. Brody sighed with relief but it was short-lived when she kissed him and whispered against his lips. "I'm having too much fun right now. Just relax. It'll be over soon." She chuckled.

"Not funny, darlin'." He raised his head to kiss her. "What about you? I want to satisfy you too."

"You can do that later. Right now deputy, you're at my mercy." She slid down his body and took him into her mouth again. Brody groaned low and long.

His hips jerked and the handcuffs pulled at his wrists. *God damn it!* She'd pay for this. He was going to pay her back ten times over. He squeezed his eyes shut as he felt his orgasm rolling over him. He barely had time to moan her name before he came. Hard. Madilyn never stopped. She suckled at him until he lay spent, her hand pumping him at the same time. Brody fell back against the pillows, feeling as if he'd just run a marathon. His chest heaved. He felt her moving up his body, kissing his stomach, chest, neck, and finally his lips.

"Please take these off now," he whispered against her lips.

She reached for the key on the nightstand and unlocked them. He rubbed his wrists.

"Did I hurt you?" she asked.

Brody blew out a laugh. "If you did, I don't remember."

Madilyn laughed as she snuggled next to him and laid her head on his chest. "I saw them and wanted to pay you back."

"You're evil as hell...and I love you for it." Brody laughed. "Remind me to hide those from you from now on."

She raised her head and gazed at him. "I liked

having you helpless for once."

"Baby, I'm always helpless around you. I have no control over my emotions when I'm around you. You're all I think of. When I close my eyes to sleep and when I wake up, it's always you."

"I love you so much, Brody. I'm so sorry for everything that happened between us."

Brody rolled to his side to face her. "It's in the past. We were both wrong. I should have discussed wanting to join the Marshals with you instead of going behind your back." He shrugged. "I thought you'd go with me no matter what."

"I should have. I never should have stood in the way of your dream." Madilyn shook her head. "When I think how I blamed Sam...I'm surprised he doesn't hate me."

"Sam understood. But we really should have talked about it. I let the love of my life slip through my fingers."

"I'm here now and we're never going to be apart again. I'll go wherever you want to go. Always. I'll never let you walk away from me again."

"I'll never walk away from you again and if you try to leave me, I'll be using those handcuffs to keep you by my side."

Madilyn laughed. "You won't need them. I'm not going anywhere without you."

"Good. Now, let's talk about getting married. It can't be soon enough for me."

"I feel the same, Brody and the rest of my life is not long enough to be with you."

Brody rolled on top of her and kissed her. "I love you so much, Maddie. Let's start our life together soon." He moved his lips to her neck and down her shoulders to her breasts. Taking a nipple into his mouth, he sucked gently as Madilyn ran her fingers through his hair. Brody moved down her body to the apex of her thighs and moved his tongue over her clitoris.

"You're so wet," he said softly.

"Turning you on turned me on," Madilyn moaned as his mouth moved over her. When his teeth scraped against her clitoris, she tried to squeeze her legs together but Brody kept them spread as he feasted on her. Madilyn raised her hips as Brody's tongue flicked at her. The orgasm tore through her. She screamed out his name and collapsed onto the bed. Brody moved up her body and gently kissed her lips.

"Payback's a bitch," he whispered, making her laugh softly. He lay down beside her and pulled her against him. They eventually fell back to sleep, both with smiles on their faces.

* * * *

Two weeks later, everyone gathered at Sam's ranch for an engagement party for Brody and Madilyn. She sat in her chair glancing around the room. She loved the people who were her friends. Hers and Brody's friends. Her eyes landed on Sam and Brody. They were laughing about something. Two gorgeous men. Madilyn glanced around again and saw Jake, Gabe, and Wyatt standing together talking with Trick and Ryder. Becca, Emma, Kaylee, Kaitlyn, and Olivia stood in a small group laughing as women do when they're together. Madilyn loved them all. She stood when she saw Kaitlyn heading toward her.

"Great turnout, huh?" Kaitlyn asked.

"It's amazing. I'm so glad we ordered more food. The cupcakes Emma made are so good, I'll gain ten pounds just looking at them." Madilyn laughed.

"I know. I've already had four of them." Kaitlyn giggled.

"I'm so happy we decided to do this. After what we went through, we needed something to make us all laugh."

Madilyn watched as Emma, Becca, and Olivia headed toward her. Kaylee moved toward her husband and Madilyn smiled as Trick automatically put his arm around his wife's waist. She saw Kaylee lean into him and Trick kissed her temple. That was love. Madilyn looked toward Brody and saw him looking at her. He winked at her making her laugh softly.

"See? That's what I want," Kaitlyn whispered.

Madilyn frowned at her. "What?"

"What you and Brody have. Kaylee and Trick. Becca and Jake. Gabe and Emma. You are all so in love. I want that someday."

"You'll have it, Katie. A man will come along and love you unconditionally."

"He'll have to accept another man's baby." Kaitlyn shook her head. "That won't be easy."

"The right man will love the baby as his own if he loves you," Madilyn told her.

"Madilyn's right, Katie," Olivia said as she moved to stand beside Katie.

Kaitlyn smiled. "I hope so, because we're going to be a package deal. Love me, love my child."

Becca put her arm around her. "If he doesn't, then he isn't the right man."

Emma smiled. "Sometimes, the right man is right in front of us. Someone we've known forever, it seems." The women laughed, drawing the gazes of everyone.

Madilyn saw Brody walking toward her. He stopped in front of her and took her hand. "I'm stealing my future bride." He grinned at the women. They smiled back as he led Madilyn away from everyone and stepped outside. He cupped her face in his hands and kissed her softly.

"I've wanted to do that for a while." He smiled at her.

Madilyn smiled up at him. "I've wanted you to." She wrapped her arms around his waist and laid her cheek on his chest. His arms wrapped around her and he rested his cheek on the top of her head. They stood there for a while not moving. Madilyn pulled back and gazed up at him. "I love you so much, Brody."

"I love you, too. It won't be too much longer and we'll be married and start our life together." He kissed the top of her head.

"It will be a good one, of that I have no doubt. We've been through so much and to finally get to this point is wonderful. I just wish I hadn't wasted those five years."

"Hush," he whispered. "It's in the past. We're here now and moving forward."

"You're right. I think we need to go back inside. It is a party for us, after all." Madilyn laughed.

Brody sighed. "If we must. I'd rather head to the barn and check out the hayloft, but I don't think Sam would appreciate it."

Madilyn burst out laughing. "We have our own barn we can check out later. Come on." She put her hand out to him and he took it. They entered the house and rejoined the party.

Epilogue

In mid-September, Madilyn sat on the edge of the tub staring at the pregnancy test strip. Positive. She took a deep breath and blew it out. They were getting married in a month. They'd decided not to have a big wedding, just close friends and family. Brody threw it together quickly. Kaitlyn would be her maid of honor and Sam would be Brody's best man. Now she had to tell him she was pregnant. How was he going to take it? Sure, they wanted children, but they'd talked about waiting so they could spend time together.

Madilyn put her hands over her face and groaned. How? Brody wore a condom every time. *They're not one hundred percent safe.* She chastised herself. Maybe she should wait until after the wedding. Not spring it on him right now. They were both so busy with work and wedding plans. She stood and nodded. She'd wait. It was the smart thing to do.

She entered the kitchen to see Brody sitting at the table with a cup of coffee in his hand. He grinned at her then frowned.

"Are you all right? You look a little pale." He stood and walked toward her.

Madilyn nodded. "I'm fine. I'm just tired. I don't think I've caught up on all the sleep I lost."

Brody nodded but continued to stare at her. "If you're sure?"

She huffed. "I'm positive, deputy. Go to work."

Brody smiled at her and kissed her forehead. "Yes, ma'am. I'll see you later. I'm glad Sam hired another deputy so I can be on days now."

"Me too. I hated not sleeping with you. Now, go." She practically pushed him out the door.

* * * *

Brody got into his truck and drove to work. Something didn't seem right with Madilyn. She was a morning person but she didn't seem like it this morning. Sighing, he pulled into the parking lot and entered the department. Betty Lou smiled up at him.

"Good morning, Brody."

"Good morning, Betty Lou. How's your morning so far?"

Betty Lou chuckled. "It's too early to tell. How about yours?"

Brody nodded. "Good. Is Sam in? I didn't see the cruiser."

"I haven't seen him yet."

"Okay. I'll talk to you later. I better get to work." Brody walked into his office and took a seat. He couldn't stop thinking about Madilyn and the way she looked this morning. He glanced up when Sam filled the doorway. "Running late, Sam?"

"I'm the sheriff. I can come in a little late if I want to." Sam grinned at him.

Brody shook his head. "I don't even want to know." He chuckled when Sam laughed.

"You and Madilyn doing all right?"

"We're both getting better every day. We're putting it behind us." Brody smiled.

Sam nodded. "Good. Glad to have you on day

shift too. I'd better get to work. I snuck in the back door so I didn't catch hell from Betty Lou for being late."

"I know you snuck in the back door, Sam Garrett, and quit swearing," Betty Lou shouted from the front office.

Brody ran his hand over his mouth as Sam muttered and walked away. Shaking his head, Brody got back to his paperwork.

* * * *

The day of the wedding was beautiful. The sun was shining down, warming the day. Madilyn sat at the kitchen table in her wedding dress. She didn't wear a traditional gown. Hers was ivory in color with sheer sleeves cuffed at her wrists with pearl buttons. A row of pearl buttons ran down the back. The bodice cinched at her waist with a sheer panel above her breasts. She glanced up when the door opened and Brody's mother, Sylvia Morgan, entered and stopped in her tracks.

"You look so beautiful, Madilyn. You can't know how happy we are that you and Brody are getting married. We've always loved you." Sylvia dabbed tears from her eyes.

Madilyn smiled up at the woman who'd been like a mother to her. "Thank you, Sylvia. I love you and Jack."

"We would love it if you called us Mom and Dad."

Madilyn blinked back tears. "I'd love to...Mom."

Sylvia choked on a sob. "We can't cry. We'll ruin our make-up. Jack's so happy to be giving you away."

Madilyn had asked Jack Morgan to give her away since she had no one else. He'd gotten tears in his eyes when he hugged her and told her he'd be more than honored.

"I know. We'd better stop. My make-up is perfect today and I refuse to ruin it," Madilyn teased.

"You do seem to be glowing today. But what bride doesn't on her wedding day?"

Madilyn nodded, but she hated lying to her future mother in-law. They'd all know soon enough. She'd even taken a second test and it also showed positive. Driving over to the next town to buy the test was the only way to get it. If she'd bought it in Clifton, it would be out already she was pregnant.

Kaitlyn strolled into the kitchen, smiling. "You look so gorgeous, Madilyn."

Madilyn smiled up at her friend. "So do you, Katie." Her eyes ran over Kaitlyn's blue gown. The color matched her beautiful eyes.

The back door opened and Jack Morgan strolled in. The man was very good-looking. He was tall like his son, black hair with streaks of gray at his temples. He winked at Sylvia, who blushed, and Madilyn knew right then, she wanted a marriage like the one they had. Still in love after thirty-four years. She stood and hugged Jack. He frowned.

"What was that for?" He smiled at her.

"Just because...Dad." She grinned up at him as he beamed.

"I like that. You've always been like a daughter

to us and I'm glad to see my son come to his senses. Now, let's get you to the church. I'm sure Brody's getting anxious." He put his arm out to her and she looped her arm through his.

Driving to the church, Madilyn smiled. The baby was a surprise, but she was happy about it. She hoped it was a boy. A little boy with dark hair and dark eyes. She knew no matter what, though, she and Brody would love this child. Hopefully, they'd have many more. Jack stopped the car at the church entrance. Madilyn stepped from the car and laughed as the crowd outside the church cheered. It was a tradition nowadays that started with Jake and Becca's wedding. She waved at them. Kaitlyn stepped out and waved. They entered the church and waited for the music to begin. Madilyn glanced around.

"He's here, don't worry," Jack whispered.

Madilyn smiled at him. "I'm not worried. I know he loves me, and he knows I love him. It's just...I wish my dad could be here."

"Oh, honey. He's here. Art's looking down on his baby girl, watching her marry the man she loves. I believe he introduced you and Brody so it would come to this. Art loved Brody."

A tear rolled down her cheek. "I know he did." She looked up. "I am marrying the man I love, Daddy. Thank you for bringing him into my life." A beam of sunlight flashed through the stained glass window beside her and moved over her. She shivered and gasped.

"I told you he was watching." Jack put his hand on her shoulder just as the wedding march began. "Let's get you married."

As they slowly moved down the aisle, Madilyn's eyes found Brody's gaze. He smiled and winked at her. She softly laughed, remembering how Jack had winked at Sylvia. Like father, like son. Jack walked her to Brody and put her hand in his. She felt Brody squeeze her hand.

"Thanks, Dad," he said to his father.

"You're welcome, son. Your mother and I are very proud of you." Jack stepped back and took a seat beside Sylvia.

Brody looked to Madilyn. "Hi, baby," he whispered.

She grinned at him. "Hi, deputy. No uniform today?"

Brody chuckled. "No, but I have the handcuffs." He sobered when he heard Sam clear his throat.

Madilyn giggled. "Wonderful."

"Could you two get married before you start the honeymoon?" Sam muttered.

Madilyn burst out laughing. "Sorry, Sam," she whispered and turned her gaze to the people in the pews. They were all smiling. She didn't think they'd heard any of the conversation but she knew they heard her laughter. She shrugged at them, making them chuckle. She then turned toward the reverend.

Feeling Brody's gaze on her, she glanced over to him. He smiled at her. "I can't believe we're finally doing this." The reverend cleared his throat. Brody chuckled. "Sorry, padre."

"You two will have years ahead of you to talk. Let me do my job," the reverend whispered.

Brody chuckled when he heard Sam laugh. The reverend sighed and continued to read from the bible. In no time, they were reciting their vows to each other and exchanging rings.

"I now pronounce you husband and wife. You may now kiss your bride," the reverend said and leaned forward. "But keep the handcuffs hidden until later."

Madilyn felt her cheeks heat up. Brody and Sam laughed, as did Kaitlyn. Madilyn laughed when Brody cupped her face in his hands and leaned in to kiss her. "And baby," she whispered.

Brody pulled back and frowned. "What?"

"I now pronounce you husband and wife...and baby," Madilyn said against his lips.

"Baby?"

She nodded. "Yes. Baby. We're having a baby." She watched his face go from shock to elation. He picked her up and let out a yell.

"Yes! We're having a baby!"

Everyone in the church cheered. When Brody set her down, she turned to hug Kaitlyn. "Looks like you and I are going through this together."

"I'm so happy for you both," Kaitlyn told her.

Madilyn and Brody turned toward the guests, linked arms, and started down the aisle. Sylvia stepped in front of them. "I knew you were glowing this morning. I'm so happy. I get to be a nana."

Madilyn and Brody hugged her and Jack then continued outside. The crowd cheered.

"We're having a baby," Brody shouted. The crowd roared.

Madilyn had never been so happy in her life.

The love of her life came back to her. He loved her and he was happy about the baby. They would begin their married life together. She moved her hand to wrap around his waist. She burst out laughing when she felt the handcuffs in his back pocket.

"I told you I had them, and I plan on keeping you cuffed to me for the rest of my life. I love you, Madilyn Morgan, more than life, and I love our baby already. Let's go start this honeymoon and then begin our life together as husband and wife."

"And baby."

"*Babies,*" Brody said. "I want babies with you."

"Anything for you, deputy. Anything. I love you, Brody. So very much. Nothing will tear us apart ever again."

"You got that right." Brody took her in his arms and pressed his lips to hers. She felt him grin when the crowd roared and Madilyn knew she would follow him wherever he roamed. Babies and all.

The End

About the Author

Susan was born and raised in Cumberland, MD. She moved to Tennessee in 1996 with her husband. She now lives in a small town outside of Nashville, along with her husband and their two rescued dogs. "JAKE" is the first book of nine in The Men of Clifton, Montana series. Although, writing for years, it was just recently she decided to submit to publishers and signed a three year contract with Secret Cravings Publishing. Since SCP closed their doors in August 2015, Susan is now with Blue Whiskey Publishing. She is a huge Nashville Predators hockey fan. She also enjoys fishing, taking drives down back roads, and visiting Gatlinburg, TN and her family in Pittsburgh, PA and her hometown. Susan also has a six book series, which started in January 2015, The Bad Boys of Dry River. Although Susan's books are a series, each book can be read as standalone books. Each book will end with a new story beginning in the next one. She would love to hear from her readers and promises to try to respond to all. She would also appreciate reviews if you've read her books.

You can visit her Facebook page and website by the links below:

https://www.facebook.com/skdromanceauthor

www.susanfisherdavisauthor.weebly.com

susan@susanfisherdavisauthor.com

Other books by Susan Fisher-Davis:

JAKE Men of Clifton, Montana Book 1
GABE Men of Clifton, Montana Book 2
LUCAS Bad Boys of Dry River, Wyoming Book 1

Made in the USA
Middletown, DE
09 May 2021